G R JORDAN

Rogues' Gallery

A Highlands and Islands Detective Thriller

First published by Carpetless Publishing 2022

Copyright © 2022 by G R Jordan

All rights reserved. No part of this publication may be reproduced, stored or transmitted in any form or by any means, electronic, mechanical, photocopying, recording, scanning, or otherwise without written permission from the publisher. It is illegal to copy this book, post it to a website, or distribute it by any other means without permission.

This novel is entirely a work of fiction. The names, characters and incidents portrayed in it are the work of the author's imagination. Any resemblance to actual persons, living or dead, events or localities is entirely coincidental.

G R Jordan asserts the moral right to be identified as the author of this work.

G R Jordan has no responsibility for the persistence or accuracy of URLs for external or third-party Internet Websites referred to in this publication and does not guarantee that any content on such Websites is, or will remain, accurate or appropriate.

Designations used by companies to distinguish their products are often claimed as trademarks. All brand names and product names used in this book and on its cover are trade names, service marks, trademarks and registered trademarks of their respective owners. The publishers and the book are not associated with any product or vendor mentioned in this book. None of the companies referenced within the book have endorsed the book.

First edition

ISBN: 978-1-915562-10-4

This book was professionally typeset on Reedsy.
Find out more at reedsy.com

Power makes you a monarch, and all the fancy robes in the world won't do the job without it.

LAURELL K HAMILTON

Contents

Foreword

The idea of one of the Scottish islands being taken as a playground for another country's rulers may seem fanciful but it provides an unique setting for Macleod where he is not the person in charge of his own investigation. As far as I know, Mingulay is not about to be bought by another country, and the imagined Zupci dynasty not about to become a major player on the world stage… as far as I know.

Acknowledgement

To Ken, Jessica, Jean, Colin, John and Rosemary for your work in bringing this novel to completion, your time and effort is deeply appreciated.

Novels by G R Jordan

The Highlands and Islands Detective series (Crime)

1. Water's Edge
2. The Bothy
3. The Horror Weekend
4. The Small Ferry
5. Dead at Third Man
6. The Pirate Club
7. A Personal Agenda
8. A Just Punishment
9. The Numerous Deaths of Santa Claus
10. Our Gated Community
11. The Satchel
12. Culhwch Alpha
13. Fair Market Value
14. The Coach Bomber
15. The Culling at Singing Sands
16. Where Justice Fails
17. The Cortado Club
18. Cleared to Die
19. Man Overboard!
20. Antisocial Behaviour
21. Rogues' Gallery
22. The Death of Macleod - Inferno Book 1

Kirsten Stewart Thrillers (Thriller)

1. A Shot at Democracy
2. The Hunted Child
3. The Express Wishes of Mr MacIver
4. The Nationalist Express
5. The Hunt for 'Red Anna'
6. The Execution of Celebrity
7. The Man Everyone Wanted
8. Busman's Holiday

The Contessa Munroe Mysteries (Cozy Mystery)

1. Corpse Reviver
2. Frostbite
3. Cobra's Fang

The Patrick Smythe Series (Crime)

1. The Disappearance of Russell Hadleigh
2. The Graves of Calgary Bay
3. The Fairy Pools Gathering

Austerley & Kirkgordon Series (Fantasy)

1. Crescendo!
2. The Darkness at Dillingham
3. Dagon's Revenge

4. Ship of Doom

Supernatural and Elder Threat Assessment Agency (SETAA) Series (Fantasy)

1. Scarlett O'Meara: Beastmaster

Island Adventures Series (Cosy Fantasy Adventure)

1. Surface Tensions

Dark Wen Series (Horror Fantasy)

1. The Blasphemous Welcome
2. The Demon's Chalice

Chapter 01

There was a faint drizzle in the air, not expected at this time of year, nor the strong wind blowing in off the sea. Julie felt that she would certainly find the conditions bracing on the island during the course that afternoon. It was a bit unusual that she'd have so few attendees. Only three were going to take part, but then again, this was a completely unusual situation. Not many instructors got hired to look after a royal party, albeit a small kingdom.

She'd never heard of Zupci, somewhere in Eastern Europe. There was that little bit in the paper about it being halved off. Some sort of dispute from the main country, but in truth, Julie didn't pay any attention to that sort of news. She was quicker into the sports pages or anything outdoors. That was her life now, and she was very happy with it.

Still, it was an unusual situation. Here she was in Mingulay, south of Barra; an island that had almost appeared to have drifted off from the rest of the Hebrides, sailing out towards the Atlantic, and yet, in so many other ways, it was like the rest of the Hebrides—rocky edges, the tight grass hanging on for dear life.

She imagined that back in the day, this must have been an

island that was perfect for kayakers to come to. Not anymore. Not since the large building had gone up in the middle of it. There was something about Mingulay being bought, this royal family from Zupci now having taken over. Of course, they weren't here all the time, but it ran like some sort of retreat for people the like of which she rarely mix with.

Occasionally, helicopters would come in and drop people off, and having been there four days, she couldn't fail to notice them. Julie had been offered a lift in the helicopter to the island due to some of the gear she required. Instead, she'd flown into Barra, the main inhabited island close by, and taken a boat down to the island in what were reasonably rough seas.

Julie was used to the weather. Used to this unseasonable roughness, and besides, it was getting her away from Matt. It was three years ago they set up their business, back when Matt and she were in love, or whatever it was. Since then, the business had flourished, but the relationship hadn't. True, she now had her own flat and didn't see him until she had to go into work. Soon the opportunity came up for an instructor to get away for a couple of weeks, train some royals in kayaking, coasteering, and a number of other outdoor sports. Julie had jumped at the chance, giving Matt no opportunity to object. She looked down at the water beneath her, turbulent, just like their relationship had been.

Taking a large gulp of sea air, Julie stood tall, looking at the rocks around her, spotting areas where it would be safe to jump into the sea, or at least crawl across the rocks and not worry if her attendees fell off. On arrival at the island, she'd taken a kayak around, skirted the edge of it, checking the lay of the land. It was almost a circle, maybe just over a kilometre in length, maybe two, but she'd been very impressed with the house that had been built in the middle of it.

Despite looking like a scar on the landscape, it had all the facilities. A connection had been run from the main island's electric supply and it seemed solid enough. She'd been given a tour of the tennis and squash courts, as well as the gym. Dinners were extravagant, but she didn't have to eat with the family. Instead, she was served in a separate room on her own, or with the servants, which was just how she liked it. They all seemed to dress so formally, and they had guests as well. She thought they were Russian, but that wasn't true, at least as she understood it. *Zupci, where on Earth is Zupci?* she thought.

Julie opened her jacket, allowing the wind to lift it up off her back. It would have blown away, except her arms were still through the sleeves. She embraced the wind as it ran over her body, giving a cooling effect. It was one of those days that if you wrapped up and worked hard, walking or climbing, you would sweat like crazy, yet when you opened up the jacket to cool down, you became cold so quickly.

She allowed herself a minute to cool before zipping up again and continuing on her way. To her left were craggy rocks, and she slowly navigated her way down, crawling across them. It seemed that she had found a decent run at last. There was a small inlet, and she'd go down in a minute and climb into the water just to see how deep it was. There didn't seem to be a significant pull out to sea and then a strong return. A quiet pool was ideal but on an island like this you took what you could get.

Julie sat down and took out a small drink that was sitting on her hip. She gulped it and made a note of where she'd have to drop down into once she got changed into her wetsuit back at the house. Normally she'd have brought everything with her,

3

but the distance in Mingulay was so short that she was quite happy to take the brief walk back and come out here dressed in the wetsuit.

Yes, this would be a good spot, she thought, looking around at the theatre of cliffs, happy that she now had a place to come to for her afternoon. She thought about who'd be coming out with her, and then she almost cursed. Pavel would be coming. The man was nineteen, but he seemed more of a boy to Julie. Julie was only twenty-five and felt younger than some of the family that she'd been educating in the various sports over these last few days.

Pavel had been a real pain. Everywhere she went, he was looking at her. Seven o'clock in the morning she'd been in the gym on the bike, having a quick half hour before she'd start the day. It'd taken her five minutes to realise he was standing at the other corner of the room, silent. He'd been behind her. She'd had her earphones in, but she suddenly got that creepy feeling that somebody was watching. When she turned to look at him, he didn't even acknowledge her and simply stared.

Two-week job, she thought, *that was all.* It was paying well, and she wasn't going to be put off by some kid. Still, she'd better get back to the house and then out here to check the depth of the water.

Julie went to turn away when she thought she saw something down by the cliff edge. The tide was coming in round the furthest point of the little inlet, and something seemed to be drifting on it. It took her only a moment to realise that it was a figure of a human, face down in the water.

Julie almost leaped in to go and save whoever it was, but she was wiser than that. She hadn't previously entered the water here and didn't know how deep it was, so she scrabbled around the rocks, clambering her way out towards the edge of the inlet.

As she got closer, she could see it was a fully-grown man, strong, powerful shoulders, along with a bare buttock that the sea kept lapping over like a floating rock. She whipped off her jacket as she got closer to the water's edge, then pulled off her leggings after kicking off her shoes. Without hesitation, she climbed into the water and struck out for the man.

As she got close, she managed to put a hand on his shoulder, but a sudden wave then pushed them both further apart. She started treading water for a moment, realising that the cold was beginning to come at her. She shouldn't have gone straight for him. She should have trodden water for a while and she rectified that issue, allowing herself to float until she was sure she had acclimatised to the water. After a minute with the body drifting further away from her, she thought she was adjusting enough to the temperature of the water to begin swimming again. She feared cramping and at least now it probably wouldn't happen.

Getting close to the man, Julie put her arm around his shoulders and started kicking with all she had, hauling him towards the rocks. It was slow work, and she could feel her energy fading, so much so that she almost cried with relief when her hand touched the rock. A sudden wave then pushed them, trapping Julie between the man and the rocks behind her. The body turned and a face with closed eyes was presented to her. She recognised the Duke of Zupci, the head of the family, someone she played tennis with only two days ago. He was a reasonably strong figure, into his fifties, she had reckoned, but he could move about the court.

As the wave subsided, Julie pulled again and managed to

5

push the man up onto the rocks while kicking out with her legs. She'd rolled him onto his back, and he lay bare to the world. Grabbing hold of a rock, she pulled herself out and began to shiver instantly. She touched his body and thought it wasn't completely cold. She put her head down on his chest but couldn't feel any rise or fall. She opened his mouth and couldn't feel his breath either.

Come on, she thought. *Come on. We need to see if we can start him up again. Think about your training, think about your training.* For ten minutes Julie went through the CPR techniques she'd been taught, fighting hard and praying that someone would come. The naked body of her current employer sprawled on the rocks with her over him performing a bizarre mouth to mouth was not the image she'd thought of that morning.

As she kept going, she suddenly had that creepy feeling again. A sudden glance up at the top of the rocks meant she saw Pavel looking down at her. There was a faint smile on the boy's lips, which was more horrific considering the fact that she was currently trying to save his father's life.

'Go get help!' she shouted at him. 'Go and get help, you stupid idiot!'

She turned back, continuing to work on the Duke, but something made her look around again. Pavel had now come closer.

'Pavel, go and get help. Your father's dying. Go get help.'

Julie saw him looking at her up and down as if he was taking in the view. She stood up. He watched as she strode over across the rocks to him. She slapped him on the shoulder.

'Go and get help. Stop looking at me and get help.'

For a moment the lad seemed to take in and assess what she was saying. Then he turned and quickly made his way up the rocks, disappearing back in the direction of the house. Julie resumed her work until ten minutes later, she sat down, exhausted. Her arms ached. Her skin was cold, goosebumps running all down her legs. Her hair tie had come loose in the water and her hair was now dripping over her shoulders.

There was a commotion at the top of the cliff, and she looked up to see some of the servants shouting. A woman was in tears. Someone came down, pushing past Julie and checking to see if the Duke was alive. Julie could tell him he wasn't. She'd tried for twenty minutes. She'd tried as hard as she could, but there was no bringing the man back. More servants arrived, then the body was lifted up and off the cliff. Julie got the sudden feeling she was alone.

She sniffed hard, sudden fearful emotions running through her. Had she done enough? Had she seen him earlier, could she have saved him? The Duke's face, so calm and sodden, kept appearing before her. That moment when she was trapped up on the rock, the wave pushing his body up and his face suddenly in front of her.

The commotion above snapped her back and she stood up because she was cold and needed to get inside. In front of her on the rocks was Pavel. He was stood in a jacket, simply looking at her.

'Give your father a hand. What the hell are you doing looking at me?'

She shook her head and started to walk up the rocks while Pavel simply watched her. As she passed him by, she stopped, turned to him and roughly unzipped his jacket. He stood almost motionless as she pulled it off his shoulders and wrapped it around her, zipping it up. It reached down to the middle of her thighs, but her bare legs were turning blue

7

from the cold. She would need to get inside, but as she reached the top of the cliffs, no one was looking at her. Instead, there was a small crowd gathered around the Duke's body.

Slowly, Julie began to trek for the house, worried that the cold would overcome her. It took the best part of five minutes to reach it, but when she did, she walked straight into the gym area, to the changing room and straight into the showers. She turned them on without even taking the coat off, allowing the water to seep over her, before she eventually stripped off. She then sat on the floor, wrapped herself up in a ball, and began to choke out tears. He was a man she'd barely known, but he'd had a good forehand. *What was he doing?* she asked herself. *What was he doing there and why, with nothing on?* Then she felt the cold still in her legs and sat huddled, allowing the water to chase away the incident from her mind.

Chapter 02

Macleod stood at the car, watching Jane carry the small picnic basket over to the wooden table. They were out in a small country park, little used, for the signage towards it was not great. Macleod thought it was perfect, somewhere for Jane to be out in the fresh air, without the hustle and bustle of people around. The hospital had said she was fine after the ordeal, at least fine physically. They'd only just returned back to their house after a month of living in a hotel and Jane was still so fragile.

Macleod struggled to recognise her for the woman that he'd fallen for. The woman who had enticed him and who between the pair of them was certainly the more outgoing. Yet having had so many delinquents running round the house, threatening her physically and sexually, only for her to be saved at the last moment by McGrath, had taken a toll on Jane that Macleod wasn't sure he'd gotten to the bottom of yet.

He watched as she took out the flask and began pouring coffee before she heard a noise. She looked up at the path, saw two men walking past. Although she gave a faint smile, Macleod could see her recoil. That was never Jane. Jane was always confident in her look and if a man cast her a glance, so what? She normally was happy with it as long as he didn't linger or make some untoward comment. She was always confident about herself, about her figure, her looks, and confident in dealing with other people. Now she was in fear.

Of course, she was putting a brave face on it. When he had brought her back to the house, Jane had said how happy she was to see the place again. When Macleod had taken her through to the patio at the rear of the house where the majority of the incident had taken place, and where certain men had exposed themselves to her, he could see Jane struggle.

Macleod walked over quickly, taking a seat beside her and putting his arm around her shoulder.

'Are you okay?' he said. 'You did well.'

'They just came from nowhere. I didn't see them. They were close.'

'Yes, they were,' said Macleod, 'but they weren't going to harm you. They weren't going to do anything. Just some walkers.'

'Yes,' she said, 'just some walkers.' She started to pour the coffee.

Macleod had wanted to go for those who had done this to Jane, but he knew the real culprits were those who had organised the raid at his house, those who had whipped it up, and he had made them pay. They were off to court. A counsellor had been exposed for the trouble he'd stirred up and his wife was facing time in jail for the murder of several people. In some ways it had been a gamble how he had brought that case to a close, but he'd done it because he was Macleod and he was good at this. One thing Seoras Macleod could be sure of was that he knew how to handle a murder investigation.

His problem now was he didn't know how to handle the fallout on his partner.

'Do you want sandwiches? Shall we have them now?' asked Jane.

'Of course, love. Whenever.' Macleod watched the ham sandwich being passed to him and he ate it slowly, thoughtfully chewing and tried not to stare at Jane.

'You can look at me,' she said. 'I know you're worried. I know you want to wrap your arms around me and take care of me. You don't have to stare away just because you think I might know this.'

'Sorry,' said Macleod and put his arm around Jane.

'Just be there for me, Seoras, understand? I know this isn't what you're good at. I don't know what I'm meant to do with it either. We just need a bit of time. Angus says we need a bit of time.'

Angus was Ross's partner, the man Macleod had struggled to meet at first. Ross, his constable, rarely spoke about his private life, but Macleod admitted that Angus had been a godsend to Jane. Macleod didn't realise that the shared act of being left at home when Ross and he went out on a case meant that Angus and Jane had a bond. The man had seemed to understand what Jane was going through and certainly got hold of the idea of how an invasion on their home would affect her. Macleod was struggling, for someone doing this to him made him stand up and fight, but he'd seen Jane lose that will.

He felt his mobile vibrate in his pocket. Macleod pulled it out to see the DCI calling him. His previous DCI had left and the one in charge at the moment was barely known to him. She had transferred up and Macleod was settling into her ways.

'Vanessa,' said Macleod. 'What can I do for you?'

'I'm sorry to do this to you, Seoras. I truly am, but we need you.'

'Need me,' said Macleod, standing up from the seat and facing away from Jane. 'You don't need me. You can't need me. I'm on leave. I'm looking after Jane. You remember what happened? I know you weren't here, but—'

'Don't,' said Vanessa. 'I'm sorry to do this to you, but this is coming from higher up. There's been a murder on Mingulay.'

'Mingulay, which one?'

'South of Barra.'

'What's that got to do with me? I mean, can Glasgow not take it?'

'No. They can't. This has come from higher up. I'm sorry, Seoras. They're insisting on you. It's some sort of diplomatic incident.'

Macleod almost began to laugh. They wanted to send him into a diplomatic situation. Diplomacy wasn't his strong point.

'Can't be done,' said Macleod. 'I'm not leaving Jane; she's too fragile.' Over his shoulder he heard Jane asking what was up. He raised his hand to indicate that he couldn't speak right now.

'It's to do with the foreign office as well. Look, I'm sorry, Seoras. I just got in today. I took a phone call. They said they want you, I don't know the ins and outs.'

'Well, it's a no; I can't leave at the moment. I've got duties. I need to care for Jane. Department owes me after what happened last time.'

'I know what happened last time and yes, I wasn't there, but clearly it's had a great effect on you and your partner, so look, just think it over and I'll be in contact. It's just a murder case on Mingulay. I'm sure you can get out there, solve it in a couple of days and get back home.'

'You said it was diplomatic, though. Mingulay?'

'The one that was bought, south of Barra, Seoras. The one that they've occupied, so to speak. It's become an island retreat, much to the annoyance of the locals.'

'Right,' said Macleod. 'I remember that from the paper, but I still don't know. I can't get down there to do that.'

'Just think on it for me, Seoras, please,' said Vanessa. 'I'm sad to say it won't be the last you hear of it.'

'Okay,' said Macleod, trying to hold back his anger. 'I know you're just following through, but make sure you tell them it's a no.'

'I will do. Take care.' The phone call was ended. Macleod stood for a moment, looking away from Jane.

'You know that bit where I said about you including me? Don't shield me from this. What's the matter?'

'They want me back. Want me off to a murder in Mingulay. Told them no.'

'Is that the new DCI doing that?' asked Jane. 'You've not really had the chance to meet her yet, have you?'

'It's from higher up. It's not her fault. You can tell, pressure is coming on her for a different reason.'

'You said no, though, didn't you?'

'Of course, I said no. I'm not leaving you at the moment. Come on, get these sandwiches eaten; we'd better be off on our walk.'

For the next three hours, Macleod and Jane strolled through a wooded forest, taking in the smell of pine and the mossy mulch that hid underneath the trees. They climbed up a large hill, following the path. Macleod thought all the talk about fresh air and exercise doing you good didn't seem to apply when coming back down the hill; your calves ached.

By the time they got back to the house, it was almost five o'clock. Macleod pulled up into the driveway of his Black Isle home and noted another car was sitting there. It was an Audi. He thought he recognised the number plate. As soon as a man stepped out of the driver's door, he knew who it was.

'Jim,' said Macleod, climbing out of the driver's side. 'What are you doing here? Or do I know?'

'Sorry to bother you at home,' said the Assistant Chief Constable. 'But I haven't really got an option on this.'

'You've met Jane, haven't you?' said Macleod, watching his partner step out of her door.

'Of course. Good to see you out and about.' Jim reached over and shook Jane's hand.

'Will you come in?' asked Jane.

'I really shouldn't impose on you.'

'It's no imposition,' said Jane. 'You work with Seoras. He told me about you, what you did in the riots on the estates. He speaks very well of you. Seoras doesn't speak like that of everyone on the force.'

'Well, no. Macleod says what he says, doesn't he?' said Jim with a smile. Jane hurried off ahead, opening the door while Macleod waited to speak quietly to Jim.

'This isn't about the Mingulay case, is it?'

'I'm afraid so, Seoras. Trouble is, it's a royal family. Have you ever heard of Zupci?'

'No,' said Macleod. 'And I don't care.'

'Well, you see, the Duke of Zupci bought Mingulay, and they turned it into their island home, or rather, their holiday home. Turns out one of the instructors there—I don't know, fitness, or sport, or something—found the Duke dead in the water.'

14

'Fine, send Hope down. McGrath can handle it. She'll have Urquhart with her as well. Between them and Ross, it's not a problem. They do most of the spade work for me, anyway. Or even better, get the DCI down. She seems to think it's important.'

'And I would happily send her, or McGrath, or even Urquhart down to it, but it's not me that's asking. It's come from higher up.'

'Higher up? What do you mean, higher up?'

'Chief Constable got a call. Got told, basically, that you were on the case. You've been requested, specifically, by the Duchess. Wants to know what happened to her husband. Turns out that Zupci have certain things that our government wants, so this is a favour being called in to them.'

'And what? I'm just meant to bow down and roll over?'

'Basically, Chief Constable is getting serious pressure on this one. Just pop down, Seoras. Couple of days and you'll be back. We'll give Jane whatever she needs.'

'You can't give Jane what she needs. She needs time, and she needs her partner with her. She needs me.'

'Are you two going to stand out there all day? I've got the kettle on,' shouted Jane from the front door. Macleod thought she seemed a little bit brighter. Maybe it was because she was doing something. Maybe it was because she knew she could trust Jim. He remembered the walkers in the park and Jane's more adverse reaction.

'He won't tell me what you've told him,' Jane said to Jim, sitting around the kitchen table. 'So kindly tell me what it is. He thinks he's protecting me, but we need to actually make decisions together.'

'You don't need to hear any of this. I've told Jim.'

15

'Even so, let me know what you've refused.'

Jim looked over at Macleod, who nodded. 'Okay, Jane, we've got a dead Duke on Mingulay, South of Barra, and his wife, the Duchess, has specifically asked for Seoras. Nothing else will do. We're in debt to them, or something or other, so the government wants this favour called in. Chief Constable is getting a lot of hassle. It's coming down the line to all of us, but let's face it, I'll back Seoras here. If you need him, Jane, he can stay.'

'Go,' said Jane.

'What do you mean, "Go," woman?' said Macleod testily. 'I'm not walking off and leaving you.'

'Go, it will be good for me. You've been coddling over me the last couple of days. I need to get back and settled into the house.'

'You're not staying on your own, though. There's no way.'

'No, I won't stay on my own.'

'We can book you a hotel and that if you want,' said Jim. 'I'm quite happy to lay out the expenses here, send you on an away trip, if you want. Go see your sisters, or brothers, or whoever you've got in the family.'

'No,' said Jane. 'I need to get back into this house and I need to get to being comfortable in it again. But I do need someone, just in case. Someone I can rely on, a friend.' Jane turned and looked at Macleod. 'Are you taking Ross with you?'

'I'm not going, but if I were going, yes, I'd take Ross with me, of course.'

'Fine. Go. Tell Angus he's staying here.'

'He's not employed by me. You need to tell him. Besides, I'm not leaving you, it's not right.'

'Give us a moment, Jim,' said Jane and watched as the

Assistant Chief Constable got up and left the room. Jane walked up and put her arms around Macleod. She smiled and kissed him on the cheek. 'You've been so good to me, but I need some room to stand on my own feet. Angus will be here. I can trust him, and you can trust him. Some bits of this, I need to do on my own. Some bits of this, you can't put a shield around me. Besides, your country needs you.'

'I'm not going off to war,' said Macleod. 'It's just some woman wants her husband's murderer found. Wants me. I'm not a dog on a chain.'

'No, but if my husband were murdered, I'd want you there. Go help somebody, Seoras. I'll be fine.'

Chapter 03

The next morning, Macleod assembled his team and took them via various flights to land on the beach of Barra, the little Twin Otter plane struggling in the wind that was making Macleod worry about the boat trip out to Mingulay. He could see the ripples on the sea, the surf as it approached the large sandy beach. When the plane trundled in towards the small terminal building, Macleod wondered if there was a helicopter to take him the short trip to Mingulay.

On arrival, he shook hands with the island's police officer and asked him if Ross could set up a base on Barra. Communications from the island could be a struggle. There was a phone line and internet at the house, but getting a signal was difficult if you were outside of the building. Macleod was also not happy that all his communications were basically running through facilities that had been set up on the island by the Duke of Zupci when he arrived. It took another two hours before the boat was ready to leave Castlebay Harbour.

On the short journey past Vatersay and down to Mingulay, Macleod sat at the rear of the boat with his case beside him, while he watched Hope standing, looking out to sea. Clarissa had decided her hair would be better served inside the wheelhouse of the boat and was currently chewing the ear of the captain. On the trip down, conversation had been muted, but there was a question on everyone's lips and Macleod knew it. Ross had got some sort of an explanation the night before when Macleod had called him to talk to Angus about coming and staying with Jane. But Hope had been good at asking about personal matters.

'You can say it if you want.'

Hope turned round and looked at Macleod. 'Say what, Seoras?'

'What you want to know.'

'You mean, why the hell are you here? Why did you just abandon your partner?'

'I didn't abandon her. She told me to go.'

'You didn't need to come. I could have covered this.'

'Something which I told the DCI and the assistant chief constable, and I told the chief constable and whoever else. I know you could cover this. You, Clarissa, Ross, you can handle it. I was told to come.'

'When are you told to do anything? That's not you. Why are you really here?'

Macleod stopped for a moment. Looked at the sea, thinking about his answer.

'Truthfully, I'm here because Jane told me to go. She wants to stand on her own two feet.'

'You think that's good? You think she's ready for that?'

'How do I know if she's ready?' Macleod stood up and walked across the small boat to stand beside McGrath. 'The thing is, Hope, when is she going to be ready? We were on a picnic the other day when two walkers just came by in the park. She nearly jumped out of her skin. She was pulling away from

19

them as if they were going to what, just flash her? She's lost all ability to rationalise around things like that. Men, especially in groups, frighten her.'

'Well, you can't blame her for that,' said Hope.

'I'm not blaming her. I'm not. I'm not even pushing her to get better quicker. It's just, this is Jane. I mean, things of that nature, she's never been shy in our relationship about it. I mean, you saw what they were doing as well.'

'Different for me, though,' said Hope. 'I didn't love the feeling that they were going to do what they wanted regardless. I'm a scrapper and I was coming to the rescue. I wasn't the one under threat.'

'You put yourself under threat the moment you jumped in. She said they were all like, waving and dangling themselves at her.'

'Yes, Seoras, I was there. I know they were. It's good if she wants to stand on her own two feet. You're sure she wasn't just trying to get you back to normal?'

'You think?' said Macleod suddenly. 'No. No, she wouldn't.'

'It's Jane you're talking about. She puts nobody else first except you.'

'No. She's not so daft. She wouldn't.'

Macleod returned to sit at the back of the boat and noticed that Clarissa was still talking inside the wheelhouse. Thankfully the wind and the door prevented him from hearing any of the conversation. He began thinking through what he'd read in his briefing that morning.

The Duke of Zupci had acquired the island, building a large house and leisure complex and was bringing people to it left, right, and centre. It had become busy. The captain of the boat had mentioned the fact that he'd done several trips out and back on most days recently. The briefing went further, going into the fact that Zupci had certain connections that the government wanted and that was why Macleod was being sent down at the request of the Duchess. It was not a formal investigation, and he was to follow the Duchess's lead. The Zupci family had diplomatic status.

She chose me by name, thought Macleod. *Why? How did the Duchess of Zupci get to know about him? After all, someone at Inverness, yes. In some ways, he was a local celebrity, or at least locally known, having been on the telly. Hope had too. Even Clarissa was getting noticed at that point.* Something about this bothered him. Why was he being asked for? Why him? Why did she know him?

Macleod watched the island approach and the new jetty that had been built since the arrival of the Duke came into view. It was an impressive structure, certainly not cheap. As they set foot onto it, Macleod thanked the captain, asking if he would remain for a while to take them back that day.

'Of course, Inspector. For the money you're paying, I'm at your discretion. Although over the next few days, it might be getting a bit rough. They say the weather's going to close in again.'

Macleod looked around him. If it hadn't closed in already, it was certainly trying. There was drizzle in the air, grey clouds all around, and looking out into the Atlantic seemed to be the bleakest option going. Why on earth would a European family want to come here on holiday? Then Macleod's mind raced. An island—it's away from everyone. Who were they?

He'd already tasked Ross with that; to dig up everything he could about the Duke of Zupci, his personal affairs and his business while Macleod went to meet the family. Macleod's case, along with Hope's and Clarissa's, were picked up but Macleod advised that they should be kept on the boat. He brought them as a precaution in case he couldn't get back, but his intention was to stay in Barra. The servant who'd been sent down to him nodded and led the way over to a small buggy.

There was only one road, if it could be called that, for it was more like a stone path that led up to the main house. The buggy, like a souped-up golf cart, drove the Inspector, Hope, and Clarissa up to the front door, where Macleod stood and admired the stonework. The house certainly hadn't been built in a hurry. As the front door opened, a smartly attired man came down and asked the Inspector to follow him, announcing that the Duchess was waiting. Macleod was led through a grand entrance hall, where he noted many paintings on the wall. He felt a tap on his shoulder as they walked across.

'Seoras,' said Clarissa, 'check the one on the left.'

Macleod looked. He saw at least three paintings which he didn't think much of, as they were mainly landscapes of some sort or other.

'They're worth at least a quarter of a million each,' said Clarissa. 'You're looking at serious money around you. The sculpture in the corner as well.'

Macleod looked over at something he couldn't actually recognise. There were twists and turns and shapes, but there was nothing discernible to him.

'You're going to tell me that's worth a quarter of a million too, aren't you,' said Macleod, raising his eyebrows.

'Half a million,' said Clarissa, with not a hint of deception on her face.

Macleod shook his head. He continued to follow the man who led him into a large sitting room.

'The Duchess will join you shortly. Can I offer any of you a drink?'

'Coffee would be good,' said Macleod.

'And for the ladies?' said the man.

'The sergeants,' said Clarissa. 'Sergeant Urquhart, Sergeant McGrath; we'll have coffee as well.'

The man turned and walked out of the door, and Macleod glowered at Clarissa. 'He didn't know. You were a bit shirty with him.'

'That's the staff, Seoras. They need to know who you are. They need to know that they're not dealing with riff-raff.'

'Well, I doubt they'll ever get that impression with you.'

Macleod looked around the room and watched as Clarissa made her way over to a painting on the wall.

'We're not on an art hunt,' said Macleod. 'Just show a bit of decorum.' Clarissa turned and looked at him, sticking her tongue out for a moment before she heard the door open behind her.

'Forgive me. I was just indisposed. I am the Duchess of Zupci, but please, you can call me Mischa.'

Macleod looked over to see a woman dressed in black. It was an elegant black, though, a dress that showed off her figure without being vulgar. There was hardly a tear in her eye, considering her husband had just died. Macleod stepped over and put out his hand. 'Detective Inspector Seoras Macleod. A pleasure to meet you, your Duchess, though such sad circumstances. They said you asked for me.'

'Indeed, I did, Inspector. Someone has killed my husband. And I want somebody who can get to the bottom of it.'

Macleod nodded. 'I'll do my best. This is—'

'That is Sergeant Hope McGrath, and beside her is Detective

23

Sergeant Clarissa Urquhart. Don't worry, I have instructed Ivan to treat you with due accord. We sometimes get people in here that, well, let's say they don't deserve to be in here.'

'Forgive me for asking,' said Macleod, 'but why me? Why am I here? I understand your husband is dead, and you have my condolences. But as far as I can gather from reading reports, it hasn't been confirmed that he was murdered yet.'

'There was a lot of bruising around the chest, but when you look closely, it wasn't the CPR that did it. He has been knifed in the chest three times. Two of which probably went through his heart.'

'And found without any clothes on in the water.'

'Yes,' sniffed the Duchess suddenly. 'A humiliation in the family. Someone is here to break up my happy home, Inspector.'

'And who exactly is here?'

'We came with my husband's mother. It's her birthday. She's over eighty, so we thought we'd better gather the family. After all, Yulia is not likely to last that much longer. So I'm here with Alexei, my son, Karina, his partner, Victor with Jenna, Pavel, my youngest son, and also Kira, my daughter. We also have some guests at the moment. Frank Smith, Lyla Preen, Sara Kurtz, Swen Drummond. People we know. And of course, we have our servants running around. There's also a Julie McGeehan. She's a sports instructor and found my husband. Unfortunately, she couldn't save him. But I guess if she hadn't been there, we wouldn't have gotten him back at all. I must thank her.'

Macleod watched the woman and saw her tears running down her cheek. She fought hard to keep them contained, pulling out a white handkerchief at times and dabbing her eyes.

'You'll need to tell me about these people who are with you, but I also want to get close to the staff just to check in case any of them have any issues with you.'

'I doubt it'd be the staff, Inspector. Most have worked for us for years. The thing about staff is they oversee each other. It doesn't do good to bite off the hand that feeds you.'

'Very good,' said Macleod. 'I'd like to talk to you all, one by one, get everyone's take on what's happening here.'

'If you wish, you can sit with me, Inspector, just not right now. You'll have to excuse me, I have got to go and attend to Yulia. She's not taking well to the death of her son. So please, feel free to have free run of the house. If you need anything, Ivan will help you.'

'That's a free rein to talk to the servants as well, I take it?'

'Of course,' said the Duchess, 'and thank you for coming.'

It was like she rose and glided across the floor to Macleod, hands out in front, grasping his. For a moment, she sniffed, and then she blurted out, 'Find them. Find whoever did this. An example must be made. An example must be made and understood.'

Chapter 04

O nce the Duchess took her leave, Macleod sent his team to work, asking Clarissa to go to talk to the staff while Hope and he would interview Julie McGeehan about finding the Duke's body. The woman was in her room and Macleod suggested that they take a walk outside, as she seemed to be agitated. Julie McGeehan was thin, at least as Macleod saw it, but he could tell she was muscly, like most people he thought of as distance runners. Strong, yet carrying no weight.

She was tall, over five foot nine, just about eclipsing Macleod, but still well short of Hope. Unlike Hope, who was quite curvaceous as well as being tall, Julie McGeehan was lithe, and every bit had the look of a sportswoman. Her face was pale, and Macleod wasn't sure that was her normal colour. He allowed Hope and himself to flank her as they took a stroll around the island of Mingulay.

'How are you feeling?' asked Macleod after giving their brief introductions.

'Quite taken aback by everything.'

'It's never nice to encounter death,' said Hope. 'We see it all the time, but it still affects us.'

'No, not just that. You see, I went in for him and I worked on him, and then they took him away. Nobody's even asked me yet how I am. I know he's family and that he's the head honcho, or he was, but not even the servants, nobody's even said anything to me.'

'How are you?' asked Macleod again.

'In shock. It was all just a bit weird.'

'Take us over to the place, if you can,' said Hope. 'We'll talk it through from there. You can say what you want. None of this will go back to the Duchess or any of the family.'

Macleod watched the woman walk slowly, at a speed that wasn't in keeping with her trim figure. He thought she'd have much more strength, but the occasion seemed to weaken her. As he approached the shore he saw her edge away, forward, towards the cliff.

'Down there,' she said. 'I was out here organising coasteering for yesterday afternoon, and I was just going to go back and get my wetsuit on and come and check the water depth. Right in the corner of my eye, I saw him. At least, something in the water. I didn't know it was him then.'

'What did you do next?' asked Hope.

'I went down to investigate. When I saw it was a figure, a man, I got in and tried to pull him across. At first, I went cold. I was stupid. I got in and tried to grab him straight away. I didn't let myself acclimatise. Once I had, I managed to pull him back over to the cliffs and I got trapped, trapped between him and the cliffs. His face was right up in front of me, and the water pulled him up. His eyes were closed. He was . . . '

'It's okay,' said Macleod. 'Try and think of some other details.'

'Well, he was naked. I remember pulling him up and turning him over, and he was just sprawled naked on the rocks. There

27

didn't seem to be any life in him. I thought, what do I do? I just started doing CPR. Did what I could. Twenty minutes, not one single breath back from him.'

'That's hard work,' said Hope. 'You must have been exhausted.'

'I was. I'm still sore today, especially my arms. But what struck me,' she said, 'is I'm working away on him and I get the feeling that somebody's watching me.'

'Really? How come?' asked Macleod.

'It's just a creepy feeling. Then I look up. Pavel's there.'

'That's the youngest son, Pavel? Eighteen or Nineteen?'

'That's him, yes. He's just looking at me. I'm working away on his dad. His dad's lying there, probably dead, nothing on, in front of him. There's me on my knees. I had been in the water, so my bottoms are off, I'm just in my top and my pants, and I'm working on him with CPR. This guy is just looking at me.'

'It must have been quite a shock for him,' said Hope.

'No, you don't understand. He was looking at me as in enjoying the view.'

'What?' blurted Macleod. 'His father's dead in front of him.'

'Pavel's been . . . , what's the best way to put this, not quite stalking me, but he's been there all the time. I do any events, Pavel's there. He says nothing. He just stares.'

'Did you mention this to anyone?'

'No. We've only been here four days and I didn't want to lose the job. They're paying incredibly well. There's some rumours that some of the items on the wall are worth a fortune, so they are a good mark.'

'What did he do then?' asked Macleod.

'That's the thing. I had to actually grab and almost shake him to go and get somebody from the house. He just kept looking, staring at me. Then, when he'd come back, the servants came down, and they can see me with the Duke down on the rocks. They grab him, they take him up off the rocks. Then I'm left there on the rocks but Pavel's just looking at me. It's just crazy. The guy's just staring at me. His father's dead, there's a whole kerfuffle around it. I walked past Pavel and got up. No, that's not right. I took his jacket off and he didn't say a word. I unzipped it, pulled it down off his shoulders, and wrapped it around me, because, frankly, I wasn't wearing a lot and he was creeping me out.'

'Then what?'

'I walked back to the house on my own, got into the shower in the changing rooms, sat in the shower, huddled up, trying to get heat back into me. My legs were blue. I was so cold.'

'Did anybody come to help you?' asked Macleod.

'No, not at all. Nobody's spoken about it. Only Ivan said to me the police were coming. That was it. But I think that's because I asked him.'

'Did you notice anything about the body? We're just trying to see why he died.'

'I didn't get much of a chance. I thought his chest looked badly bruised, although that may have been afterwards, by the time I'd worked on him. They tell you to be quite heavy-handed with the CPR, so I was.'

'Outside of Pavel, has anyone else been weird with you?'

'No,' said Julie. 'I mean, I've done sports with most of the men and they're all quite keen to do it. You get glances, glimpses and that, but nobody's been inappropriate. Nobody's asked for anything and they've been detached outside of my activities. The staff don't really want to know me, but that's okay. I keep myself to myself. I'm here for two weeks doing a job, but Pavel has come to everything I've organised. Said nothing and watched. I'm finding him a bit weird, but to be honest, I think if he did try anything, I could handle him all right. I just didn't want to rock the boat. And then this happened. I did think, should I leave? But then you were coming. They said you'd want to speak to me. I offered to stay in Barra, but they said no, because there'd be more activities to organise. We still had guests. The man's just died so I don't get that. I don't get why things seem to be carrying on as normal.'

'What do you mean, normal?' asked Hope.

'Well, that's the thing. There are some younger kids running around. I've done a bit of work with them. I've done a bit of work with the older people too. The guests that have come haven't really participated with me, but that's all right. I take whoever comes along. But I thought they'd have headed home unless you stopped them from heading anywhere.'

'Wasn't me,' said Macleod. 'Although I would now. You said Pavel follows you. Has he asked for anything from you or indicated anything else?'

'No, but when I see him, I don't think he's that well-liked by the family. His father didn't seem that enamoured with him. He seemed closer to Alexei and Victor.'

'Did you notice any animosity amongst the family?'

'To be honest, I just get on with my business and keep well out of that. I had enough to do planning things. As I said, I'm here for two weeks to keep them entertained on a sports front. That's it.'

Macleod thanked the woman. He walked back with her towards the house, the faint drizzle still falling. Macleod felt the wind was beginning to pick up and he hoped the water wouldn't get choppier on the way back to Barra tonight. As he reached the house, he asked Ivan, one of the servants, if any of the rest of his team had arrived.

'A Japanese lady has arrived, sir. She's set up in a room at the back. Let me take you through.'

Ivan marched Macleod and Hope past the kitchens into an outhouse, which was cold. Inside on the table lay a body with a blanket over it and Macleod saw Jona Nakamura in the far corner. She turned and welcomed them before waiting for Ivan to leave the room.

'I'm not stopping here,' said Jona. 'I'm going to take the body back to Barra. Got a few better facilities there I can work with, but you might want to take a look at this first.' Jona pulled back the cover and Macleod looked at the silent body of the Duke of Zupci.

'See the chest?' said Jona. 'Heavy bruising. Yes, there was CPR on it, but if you look closely, there's actually three knife wounds. Brutally good knife, clean as a whistle. Two cuts into the heart, other one missed it. Looking at them, probably done with extreme force from above him. I would say he might even have been lying on his back, given the angle of attack. Otherwise, he's going to have somebody that's much taller than him coming down and in. More consistent, he's on his back when he's killed. I'll see if I can get any further, but at the moment, I just need to get packed up and back to Barra. The crime scene I take it probably isn't worth looking at?'

'We haven't got a crime scene,' said Macleod. 'We've got a body in the water. So, no, I can't help you with that one, but don't take the boat back until we're there. I need to get back off island and have a think about what's going on. I also want to get an idea from Ross about this family before we interview

31

them too much.'

Having left Jona, Macleod rounded up Clarissa. He insisted on them going outside to speak, back out in the drizzle. Macleod wrapped his coat around him, feeling cold despite the time of year.

'Why are we out here?' asked Macleod.

'Well, you said to step outside,' said Hope

'No, why are we on the island?'

Clarissa looked up at Macleod and McGrath. 'Simple thing is, the staff don't want to talk. There's a silence going around amongst them all. Even when I asked about finding the body, I had to drag it out of them. Who was there? Who picked him up? What they did with him? It all seems fine though. They brought him back here. He'd been left in the room and Jona's now seeing him.

'But when I ask about the family, there's not a word. Just very nice people basically. I don't believe that for a minute. It seems to me like I've got frightened rats, all worried that the master's going to dump them if they say anything. Well, who the master is, who knows now the Duke's dead. I tried asking about that. I got a wall of silence. I don't know how they do it over there. Do the males rule? Do they swap it about with the men and the women?'

'What do you mean?' asked Macleod.

'Well, they are royalty, so who succeeds. I also asked about Yulia. She's almost revered here by the servants. It's hard because as I say, they don't say a bad word about any of them, but particularly about Yulia.'

Macleod looked around him and thought even for the time of year, it was starting to get dark. He certainly didn't fancy making his way back over in failing light.

'Tomorrow, we pull them all in. We get back over here early and we talk to everyone on the island. I want to go back and get a brief from Ross tonight. I don't like going in and not knowing who I'm talking to. Make sure we have the names of all the guests, the names of all the staff. We get that all run through tonight, we come back here, and we go at it tomorrow. Hopefully, we get the body back, Jona will have an idea of roughly when he was killed as well.'

'I'll get on it and get the detail then,' said Clarissa, and left McGrath with Macleod.

'What's up, Seoras? You've got that look on your face. You're bothered by something.'

'I'm bothered by it all. Think of it, Hope. I come down here, well I'm requested to come. When I get here, I've got a servant class that won't speak ill of anybody. I've got a random set of visitors. Somebody in his own holiday home is done away with. Look around here too. No security. If they're so high up and such royalty or whatever they're meant to be, where's the security? Why is no one here? Why haven't they got their own people to investigate this? If that was me, I probably wouldn't even call the police in.'

'She didn't, she asked for you.'

'There's something about this I'm not liking. It's just a feeling. A feeling that something else isn't right here. All those paintings, the cost. Where's the security? What's to stop somebody just coming over here and running riot, taking everything?'

'Maybe nobody knows. Staff are all tight knit. Visitors, maybe they're kosher.'

'Well, something isn't,' said Macleod. 'Something isn't kosher.'

Chapter 05

ope knocked on Macleod's door at the small hotel in Castlebay and remembered an earlier time when they had stayed there. Kirsten Stewart had been with them in a case where people were being murdered in a hunt for a stolen item that had been hidden in a cryptic fashion. It had stretched across a couple of the smaller isles and Hope thought about it favourably, almost fondly, as the early days of forging her friendship with Macleod. As she waited at the door, she heard him trying to console Jane at the other end of the phone. Maybe she'd had a rough day, who knew, but Macleod's mood was not great.

It bothered him coming away and yet Hope thought he knew that he couldn't protect Jane forever. She'd have to come to her terms with the event that had happened and although it had shocked Hope, she was built differently, ready to turn around and lash out hard at those who were trying to force anything upon her. Jane, for being such a vivacious woman, struggled to deal with that intensity of unsocial behaviour. Hope chewed the word around in her head. Such a polite phrase for something that was so gross and invasive.

The door opened, Macleod still on the phone, and he

motioned Hope to sit down in the chair opposite a table. When she'd done so, he pointed over to the kettle and then to a couple of cups. When she'd first met him, such an action would've annoyed her, as if she was some sort of a tea lady, but not now. Things concerned with coffee just happened automatically with him, as if he seemed to live off it, an inner fuel second only to air and water.

As Macleod signed off on the phone with Jane, Hope poured the water and made the instant coffee and saw Macleod's face as he then picked up one of the packets. It would have to do for there was no other choice. He sat down, taking the cup from Hope, thanking her.

'How's she doing?' asked Hope.

'She had a bit of a rough day. Had a moment outside when, well, let's just say it all came flooding back.'

'Was she on her own?'

'Angus was inside,' said Macleod. 'Good job, too. He's been very kind to her. I don't know why, but they really do seem to hit it off. Anyway, did you organise the room downstairs?'

'I didn't need to. Ross has it all under control as ever. He says to come down in about ten minutes. He's got that look on his face.'

'That look?' queried Macleod.

'Yes. The one where he's excited about something. When he's found things out, he always tries to look professional, but there's like a little kid inside bubbling over with enthusiasm to tell his parents what he's done.' Macleod looked over at Hope.

'I'm not sure the analogy works that well. I certainly don't see us as his parents.'

'Don't you?' asked Hope. 'You always seem like a father figure to him.'

35

Macleod shook his head. 'We've really got to put you to work on better descriptions. Anyway, how are you and the rest of the team?'

'We're fine. We weren't the ones that got ripped away from a loved one.'

'No,' said Macleod, 'but it's easier to think about other people at the moment. It's there all the time gnawing at me, wondering how she is, how she's getting on, and I don't want to phone because if I phone too often, she'll complain that I'm not letting her get on with it, trying to discover how well she is. It's not easy standing at a distance.'

'No, it's not,' said Hope. 'Still hurts that they didn't let me take this job.'

'Don't feel like that,' said Macleod. 'It's just this diplomatic stuff. I mean, I don't understand it fully, but . . . '

His mobile phone rang and Macleod picked it up and looked at the number displayed on the screen. 'This is what I'm talking about. The Assistant Chief Constable.'

'I'll see you downstairs,' said Hope, taking her coffee with her. 'Don't be too grumpy with him.'

Macleod rolled his eyes at her as she walked past and then pressed the green button and accepted the call.

'Seoras, how's it going?'

Jim almost sounded chipper, but then his tone changed somewhat before Macleod could answer. 'They're asking, they're asking big time. Keep getting told that it's our investigation and they're not going to interfere, but they're on the phone all the time. They want this cleared up in a nice way. Find out which servants did it. That's the tone coming down from up on high.'

'Hold on a minute,' said Macleod. 'Who said the servants did it? We're only just there, still getting the lay of the land.'

'There's been some rumour put out that the sports instructor did it. She found him, didn't she?'

'Yes, she did. But it's not helpful if people make accusations from afar. Nobody here has accused her. In fact, they seemed to have ignored her.'

'Well, that's where all the song and dance is coming from in the diplomatic channels; just passing it on. Not sure on the servants' status, either. Immunity and that.'

'Stop right there, Jim. Just stop right there. I'm not taking this. I know it's you, but you tell them I get a free run of this or I'm walking. I get nonsense like that coming down from above, I'll step out. I've got every reason to. They want to cajole me to come down here, they want to put pressure on, fine. I'll put pressure back. They let me be. I've got my team and we'll get to the bottom of it, but they need to leave me alone. I work best when left to it.'

'I know that,' said Jim, 'but that's not going to fly.'

'Then make it fly, Jim. You make it fly.'

Macleod was almost surprised by his own tone, and it caused him to stand up out of his chair. One of his hands swung around in frustration and he watched the coffee cup tip over, the brown liquid running down the side of the unit.

'Easy, Seoras. You don't need to threaten me.'

'Sorry,' said Macleod. 'I know I don't, but you need to go to battle on this. You need to kick back. Tell the Chief Constable to kick back. We're not here to get dragged all over the place. We deal with crime. We solve it. We put it to the proper authorities to prosecute.'

'With the diplomatic community involved in this one, that might be hard to do. Just concentrate on solving it,' said Jim.

'I'll take what flack I can off you, but do me a favour. Keep the updates coming. Makes it easier for me to put that umbrella above you.'

'Understood,' said Macleod. 'I need to go, Jim. Got a briefing with the team.'

'Okay, and how's she doing?'

'Doing? She's doing . . . I don't know how she's doing.'

Macleod closed the call before Jim could answer. He looked at the coffee cup strewn on the carpet and turned on his heel, walking out the door slowly to the briefing room Ross had set up. They had commandeered two of the rooms of the hotel, which had an interconnecting door. One had been set up with a small team of Ross's, trying to take in what detail they could about the Duke of Zupci. The other room had a small, round table in it.

When Macleod entered, he saw his team sitting around the table. In the far corner was a coffee machine, not a kettle. Macleod noted it was an actual filter coffee machine. He wandered over and looked at the coffee sitting beside it. There was a grinder too. *How did Ross do this?* he asked himself. *Everywhere we go, he's so organised. Where did he dig up a grinder from here?*

'Coffee's in the jug, sir,' said Ross, beaming over at Macleod and Hope's idea of the son trying to impress his father came back to Macleod. It wasn't an idea he wanted in his head.

'Thank you, Ross. What sort of . . .?'

'Coffee is it, sir? It's the same one you have at the station. I know you like it. Packed some with us.'

Sometimes Hope's comments were close to the bone. Macleod smiled, poured his coffee, and sat down at the table.

'Okay,' said Macleod. 'Tomorrow, we go and interview all of

38

these people. Ross is going to run through them, tell us who's who just so we all know where we're starting from. Once he's done that, we'll work out who's interviewing who tomorrow.' Macleod yawned.

'It's been a long day, Seoras, hasn't it?' said Clarissa.

'It has,' said Macleod. 'Let's get on. Go on, Ross; nothing superfluous.'

Macleod looked over and saw Ross almost looking hurt. When did he ever throw in anything superfluous?

'Mingulay was bought a couple of years ago by the Duke of Zupci in a rather angry purchase. The locals weren't happy and especially weren't happy when he built this holiday home. Zupci is a break-off faction of an Eastern European state. It's not that big, but it's been causing issues with the former government and also other parts of the world. We believe there's a lot of drugs and other nefarious items passing through that country on the way to elsewhere. However, they do have certain items and information available which may be why our government is willing to work with them.'

'Nice,' said Clarissa.

'Any information on the heightened danger to us,' said Macleod, 'given the status of the small country?'

'No,' said Ross. 'They also invited us in. I do genuinely think that they want us to be there. From the top. Deceased man was the Duke of Zupci. He was head of a family of three sons and a daughter. He has a mother who is also at the island. Her name is Yulia, but she seems to have taken a back role in the last twenty years. The Duke was in charge when the kingdom was divided from its parent country a few years ago. The political wheelings and dealings to make that happen have been described by our foreign office as, frankly, impressive. A lot is attributed to the man.

'He has a wife—I'm sorry, he has a widow called Mischa. They used to have a common surname, but they now take Zupci as an active surname. Between them, they have three sons. Alexei is the oldest, who seems to have been following in the father's footsteps. We believe he runs small areas of the business for him. He's married to Karina Jones, formerly Karen Jones. She's an American. That's what little is known. The second son is Victor. He tends to lead a rather raucous lifestyle. Bit of a playboy. His partner is Jenna Arquette, who is a former model of the glamour variety. A lot of people have described her as a trophy girlfriend. She has been with him for a couple of years now. The youngest son is Pavel.'

'Julie McGeehan said he was following her around,' interrupted Hope.

'What little contact I've had with the state has described him as an upright member of the family who has achieved many great things. When I talked to the parent country's attaché, he kind of poo-pooed that.'

'What do you mean, he kind of poo-pooed that?'

'Well, sir, he said basically that he was a . . .'

'What?' asked Macleod. 'What did he say?'

Ross looked embarrassed. 'Said he was an arsehole, sir. Useless arsehole.'

Macleod gave his head a slight shake.

'Beginning to like the former country,' said Clarissa.

'There is one other member of the family,' said Ross. 'Kira, she's only just turned sixteen. Younger daughter. Very little known about her. According to my attaché, they say she's . . .'

'Keep it clean,' said Macleod.

'They said she's in her mother's footsteps,' said Ross, smiling.

40

'Always seen around her mother. Quite a timid thing. You don't want to know what the Zupci official said about her. Nobody could be that good.'

'What else do we know about them?' asked Macleod.

'Only that they're worth a fortune,' said Ross.

'I told you that, didn't I?' said Clarissa. 'Paintings, sculptures in there. I totalled over £12 million worth, and that's the holiday home. So why are we here, Seoras? If they can afford that amount of money, they could have hired in anyone. Why would you want a Scottish plod?'

Macleod looked over at Clarissa. 'Thank you for that. A Scottish plod? I like to think I'm a little bit more than that.'

'You know what I'm saying.'

'She's right,' said Hope. 'In all of this, the money, everything else, we need to keep our eye out as to why we're here. Surely they could have dealt with it.'

'There's no security,' said Macleod. 'There's no security. They're a royal family. Unless those servants are the security and they're hiding under the cover of being a servant, there's no security.'

'What does that mean?' asked Clarissa.

'I don't know,' said Macleod, 'but Hope's right.'

'They've also got guests with them, of course,' said Ross. 'I've done a bit of work on them. Frank Schmidt's a German businessman. I know he's had dealings with the family. Some of our German colleagues have been tracing him for years, but they're having a hard time pinning anything on him. He's a crack operator, but he's also a nasty figure. Lyla Preen is an actress, although how she got her acting jobs remains to be clarified in full. She operates with high rollers, been seen with the mighty and also the deeply dubious in this world. Sarah

Kurtz is a former model. Again, not the sort that would go on the catwalk, a different sort of model.'

'Clarify,' said Macleod.

'Glamour models, sir. The kind that gets their . . .'

'I know what it means,' Macleod said to Clarissa. 'Why is she here?'

'Why do you think she's here? Somebody's probably giving her paymaster . . . ' Macleod rolled his eyes at Clarissa. 'A very good time,' she said pointedly.

'There does seem to be a rather fancy collection of women around the men,' said Hope.

'It seems to me we've got a rogues' gallery,' said Macleod. 'There doesn't seem to be anybody squeaky clean here.'

'With the possible exception of Kira,' said Ross. 'I can't find anything on her.'

'She's sixteen,' said Clarissa. 'Give her a chance. Although by sixteen, I had . . .'

'We don't need to know about your previous life, or conquests,' said Macleod. 'In short, Ross, what have we got?'

'We've got a family with many dubious connections—nothing of which has been proved—that's come to prominence in a country where really they're wondering quite how they did it. They've got guests around them that mix with the rich and the famous and do dealings in the dark. I'll take your description of that, a rogues' gallery. The amazing thing is when I spoke to the Zupci police, everybody on that list had a perfect report. Frankly, I wouldn't trust anything that comes out of the Zupci police offices.'

'Somebody decided to kill the head honcho. More than that,' said Macleod, 'they killed him and left him naked in the sea. We go tomorrow, we take them all aside into rooms and we

42

put the squeeze on them. I don't think it's going to be easy because these guys seem to be operators. Where's Jona, by the way?'

'Working on our body,' said Ross. 'She'll tell you when she's got something. She's operating out at the cottage hospital.'

'Has she got everything?' asked Hope.

'I believe so,' said Ross. 'At least, she hasn't asked for anything else.'

'Just let her be to get on with it,' said Macleod. 'One other thing, don't rush this.'

'How do you mean, Seoras?' asked Clarissa.

'What'd I say? Don't rush this. Walk into this with your eyes open. Why are we here? Every time, why are we here? I know you all think I want to be back up the road tout de suite, but this is a job like any other. Well, maybe not like every other, but it's still a job for this team and we will be thorough.'

He stretched forward, took his coffee cup, and drained the last of it. Placing it back on the table, he looked around at the team. 'Business dealings, where they've come from, what are the links to the family? What have they done over the last five years? Why are they really here? Where were they when our friend died? Do we have a time scale or not yet?'

'Sometime in the middle of the night, just working to try and narrow it down,' said Ross.

Macleod nodded. 'All right, then, so it's who's in bed with who, really, isn't it?'

'The servants too,' said Clarissa. 'You want the servants treated in the same way.'

'I will do but we start with the family and the guests.'

'People like this, they keep their servants in line, sir,' said Ross. 'Just one last thing. Swen Drummond, the fourth guest.

43

He's a rather shadowy figure. They didn't have a lot on him, but Swedish police think he's a possible hitman.'

'At which point were you going to tell me that? Actually, we could all be at risk.'

'I don't think we're at risk, sir,' said Ross. 'The thing about hitmen is they take out who they're paid to. Everyone else costs extra.'

'Well, that's a comforting thought,' said Hope. 'Still, it will be worth watching him for whatever reason he is here.'

'Not like a hitman to advertise where he is,' said Macleod. 'Okay, go get some rest, everyone. Early start in the morning. Make sure we pack some small bags to take with us. The way the weather's shaping up, it might be a long stay over. I'm not sure the boat will run.' Macleod stood up and the rest of his team joined him, Ross starting to clear away the cups.

'Just leave them, Alan,' said Hope. 'We'll get some in the morning before we head off.' Macleod watched Ross and Clarissa leave the room before turning to Hope.

'You're right. Why are we here? Why are we here, Hope?'

'I don't know,' she said, 'but it's making me uneasy.'

'I'll tell you what though,' said Macleod. 'We solve that, we solve this. There's too much pressure surrounding this, there's too much push for me to be here. You're spot on, Hope; you're spot on.' She patted him on the back as he walked through the door.

'Trained by the best, Seoras; trained by the best.'

44

Chapter 06

'I wouldn't be too late tonight, Detective Inspector. D'you see it? It'll be coming in later. The swell will pick up. I doubt I'll be able to get back out for you. I've got some stuff I need to do so I won't be hanging around either.'

'That's understood,' said Macleod. 'I grew up in Lewis. I know what the weather's like out this way.'

'Macleod, I should have guessed. Although the names have changed recently.' The captain of the vessel gave a grimace and turned back to the wheel. 'Best if you sit down, Inspector, may be a bit rough on the way over. In fact, tell them all to sit down except for that Sergeant of yours. She said she wanted to see more how the boat handled today.'

'Detective Sergeant Urquhart?' said Macleod.

'Clarissa was her name, least that's what she told me. Not a name you hear that often, is it?'

'No, it's not. Are you happy enough having her up there? You don't have to. I pay you to take us over to the island, not explain the ins and outs of how to pilot a vessel.'

'Oh, she's fine. Tell her to pop up when she's ready.'

Macleod exited the wheelhouse, found himself a seat to the rear of the boat beside Hope and motioned to Clarissa to go into the wheelhouse. She seemed extremely eager and as the boat made its way across what was already a choppy sea, Macleod watched her talk endlessly to the captain.

'I didn't know she was the sailing type,' said Ross.

'I don't think it's the water she's after,' said Hope.

'She's at that stage of life, isn't she?' said Macleod.

'And what is that meant to mean?' asked Hope.

'I didn't mean anything by it. I mean, she's on her own. She's seen that life's not got that much further ahead. There's more behind now than there is in front and you think, am I spending it on my own? I didn't mean anything to do with being a woman.'

'Just be thankful you're attached,' she said.

Macleod frowned for a moment and then looked at Hope, wondering if she was being serious with that comment. He decided to ignore any further exploration of it and looked out, watching the sea bounce up and down and remembering his days of fishing, back when he was younger. It always took a while to get used to the boat swaying this way and that, but once you did, there was nothing quite like the waters around here.

He remembered when he used to see the whales coming up, the dolphins jumping in and out. Of course, it was all work. They were out fishing, but the sights you saw along the way were quite something.

The island appeared, looking dour in the grey light, and once again the party was greeted by a servant sent from the house. There was only one other person outdoors Macleod could see, Julie McGeehan running around the island, obviously deciding keeping fit was a way of handling the situation that had gone on. He didn't blame her. She'd be out of the house, away from

46

the people she said had treated her so coldly.

As the little buggy drove him up to the house, Macleod was planning in his head where everyone should go. Clarissa would stay working with the servants and then pick up the guests, while Macleod and Hope would deal with the family on arrival.

Ivan, the main manservant, stepped out to greet Macleod without a 'hello'. A smile wouldn't have gone amiss.

'How can I help you today, Detective Inspector?' the man said impassively.

'I'd like a separate room for each of the family and their guests. I'm going to need to interview them, but not together. I don't want to detain them as if we were in a station or that. If they could confine themselves to an area of the house or a room, then I could easily visit them there to interview without stopping all their movement.'

'I don't believe that's the way the mistress wants it done.'

Macleod stopped, found himself almost having to reset to comprehend the comment, and then looked at Ivan. 'That's the way I want it done. I'm being quite good here. I could pull everybody back to Barra and into the station. Someone has died.'

'I'm very well aware of that, sir. The master is dead and I'm aware you're here to find out who dispatched him, but the mistress of the house doesn't want life to be overly disturbed.'

'Maybe you can inform the mistress that I'm running a murder investigation, and this is what's going to happen.'

Macleod saw Ivan tremble. It was the first time he'd seen it in the man. He was so professional, cool, detached, and yet with that one comment, the man seemed to shake.

'How about I tell her, Ivan? Maybe you'd be so good as to show me where she is.'

47

'The mistress is getting changed at the moment. If I could escort you into the drawing room, you could await her arrival.'

'I'm running a murder investigation, Ivan. I come, I organise the timetable, I set the agenda. Kindly go and get your mistress for me.'

'Very good, sir,' said Ivan, but clearly it wasn't good for him at all. That little shake had come back in, as if he knew he was about to do something extremely unpalatable.

Despite this, Ivan showed the team to the drawing room where they waited for the next twenty minutes. Clarissa was obsessed with the artwork around her and after the third mention of how much one of the paintings cost, Macleod put his hand up in annoyance. He wasn't used to being kept waiting and he didn't need to be reminded that there was money driving this. Money that said everybody could wait for them.

Now, money didn't move the world; people did. Decency and respect did. That's what really got on, wasn't it? It had to be. It must be.

The door opened suddenly and a voice from the other side said, 'Maybe your people could leave.' There was no formality. Macleod turned to Hope, giving her a nod. She exited with Clarissa and Ross, and Macleod turned to face the door while the Duchess of Zupci entered the room. She had a dressing gown on, and her face was indignant.

'Why do you interrupt me? I was in the middle of my bath.'

'I'm sorry to disturb you, but I've been informed by your manservant my way of running an investigation isn't palatable to you,' said Macleod, turning away from the woman.

'There's no need to insult me, to turn your back on me.' Macleod turned back around.

'My apologies,' he said calmly, 'but where I come from, when a woman comes in in a state of undress, it's polite for a man to look the other way.'

'I'm not in undress,' said Mischa. 'Where I come from, a woman would rather be admired than ignored. What is it that you want of me?' she said.

'I want to run an investigation. I want all of your guests in a separate room in the house or give me one single room and bring them in one at a time. Your husband was murdered, ma'am. I need to find out who did it. You asked for me. Here I am, despite my own issues at home.'

'Your wife, Jane, how is she doing? Terrible incident, wasn't it? Must be difficult for you not being able to do what you want to those people who injured your wife in such a way. Mental injuries are the hardest to come back from. I bet you wanted to castrate them, like cattle.'

Macleod could feel the blood boiling in him, and he fought to control himself. Who did she think she was, bringing up his personal life? He was the detective here. Not some play toy.

'I'm going to run an investigation and I'd like you to follow it.'

'You simply walk around and ask people questions. These are my guests. I cannot hold them. To even show that we suspect them would be bad for them. Some in my country might react; it would put their lives in danger.'

'I've looked at your guests and I would suspect every one of them,' said Macleod. 'Frankly, I suspect most of your family as well.'

The woman stepped forward, walking up to Macleod and slapped him across the cheek.

Macleod was taken aback, but he rallied magnificently. 'One

more time, I walk. You wanted me here for a reason. I'm here. I need some cooperation.'

'I'm sorry,' said Mischa, eyes narrowing at Macleod, 'but when people insult my family back home, we deal with it.'

'I'm sure you do, but somebody here killed your husband. And as you've dragged me here, I intend to get to the bottom of it.'

'You'll do that without turning this into a police station,' said Mischa. 'I think you'll find your government will back me on that one. I expect you to operate more discreetly.'

Macleod got the feeling that this woman thought she was his boss. Maybe being so powerful, she just expected those around her to act according to her wishes.

'Does the Zupci police follow your orders?'

'They do as told. Small men do,' said the woman indignantly.

'I'm sure they do. However, I am a Detective Inspector in the Scottish police force and I will conduct this investigation as I see fit.'

Mischa turned on her heel, marched over to telephone, picked it up and dialled a number. She spoke in Russian before slamming the phone down. She then stood off to the window, looking out, ignoring Macleod. Two minutes later, the door was rapped. Mischa told Ivan to come in. The man appeared with a telephone and handed it to the inspector.

'It's for you, sir. I believe it's the foreign secretary.'

Macleod narrowed his eyes at the phone. He picked it up. 'Are you the foreign secretary?' asked Macleod.

'This is James Bartholomew, foreign secretary.' Without hesitation, Macleod switched the phone off, handed it back to Ivan, who nodded and took it away. Part of Macleod wanted to walk. They weren't playing by his rules. They weren't playing fair at all. She wanted him there. She should follow his methods, his way, but something was afoot. This was a mystery, a murder, and every core of his fibre was going to solve it. Whatever way he had to run around to do it. He strode over to Mischa at the window.

'Okay. You get your way, but I'll get to the bottom of this. Expect to be talking to me today.' Before she could react, Macleod left the room and walked straight into a set of eager faces.

'What was that all about?' asked Hope. 'You were in there for ages.'

'Received a call from the foreign office. It appears we're going to have to do this a little bit differently. I want you to get close to them all. Fan out. Don't hold back on your questions either. Something's going on here. Something beyond the norm.'

'Okay. Who do we take first?' Before Macleod could answer, a telephone was brought to him again by Ivan.

'Hope this isn't the foreign secretary again. I'm not in a good mood with him, Ivan,' said Macleod. The man's face was impassive. Macleod took the phone, finding Jona on the other end of the line.

'Inspector, just to let you know, the Duke was killed with multiple stab wounds. Three, we believe, two of which pierced the heart.'

'That's pretty vicious. Like those of a hit man. We've got one of them on the island.'

'No,' said Jona, 'this is the thing. There was no struggle from him. There's no holding down wrists. There's no—well, nothing really. There's bruising from where he had CPR work done on him on his chest. But prior to that, there were three knife wounds. You're looking for a thin weapon. The blade is approximately six inches long.'

'Anything else you can tell me about it?'

'From the entry position, the person would have to be about six feet tall because the blade goes in almost straight—that's if he was standing. My guess would be, he was lying on his back at the time. In which case, someone on top could have plunged the blade in. It's almost perpendicular to the chest. If anything, it's coming in from a slightly more acute angle than that. In from the top, not from the bottom.'

'Somebody, what, astride him? Is that what you're saying, Jona?'

'That would be my best guess,' she said. 'No struggle marks. Someone he knew.'

Macleod thanked her and gave the phone back to Ivan. Once he departed, Macleod turned to his colleagues and advised them of Jona's finding.

'Someone he knew,' said Clarissa. 'He knows everybody on this island. Isn't that the point of having guests?'

'I don't think the forensics are going to break this one,' said Macleod. 'This is going to be about getting underneath these people and trying to get to how they work. Hope, go and speak to the eldest son. I'm going to take Yulia, Mischa and her daughter. Ross, you come with me. Clarissa, see what you can find out about the rest of the family.'

Chapter 07

H ope found Ivan and asked the servant where Alexei and Karina were. He advised her to follow him down several steps and through the house, out towards the rear where there would be an indoor pool area. He said that usually they occupied there or somewhere around the steam rooms. He offered to show Hope the way, but she declined and strolled through the house, looking around at the numerous items on the wall or displayed on little stands. Each had its own light at the top showing the item off in its best light.

Hope wandered down several flights of stairs and then found herself at what seemed to be a large pool with a glass canopy covering it. There was no sunlight blazing in today because the weather outside was dark and foreboding, so lights at the side of the pool lit it up. She counted five lanes and admired the underwater lights that gave the pool a warm look. As she stood admiring it, a voice called to her from the other side of the room.

'Are you with that inspector?'

She turned to see a tall man, reasonably broad with dark hair and Hope clocked him to be quite handsome. He was still in a pair of swimming trunks, the tight variety preferred by Europeans, and she strolled around the pool towards him before answering.

'My name is Detective Sergeant Hope McGrath, and I'm part of Detective Inspector Macleod's team. I'd like to ask you a few questions regarding the death of the Duke of Zupci. My condolences on the death of your father. I take it you're Alexei.'

'I am. No doubt you've done your homework on me.'

'No more than anyone else,' said Hope. 'I just need to ask you a few questions about what was going on, whether your father had any enemies and that sort of thing.'

'I'm just about to go in for my sauna, so please, you're welcome to come and join me. I'm sure we could find you a towel.'

Hope by now was realising the man was eyeing her up when she took off her leather jacket, placing it down on the sun lounger by the pool.

'I'll be fine just like this,' she said. 'Please lead the way.'

The man turned and walked towards a wooden cabin at the rear of the pool and opened the door, inviting Hope inside. Her hair was already tied up, but she pulled her T-shirt out from her skin as she felt the hot air begin to hit her. Hope was very fair in her complexion, and while she did sunbathe, she wasn't too keen on a lot of heat, especially this moist kind. Hope had only just taken a seat on the bottom level of the sauna before she realised there was a woman at the top, lying down.

'This is my wife, Karina,' said Alexei. The blonde-haired woman rose up into a sitting position at the top. She clearly had been in for a while, for the sweat was pouring off her face, but she had a towel tucked around her.

'Do you want a towel, my dear?' said the woman in a light

American accent.

'I'm fine,' said Hope, as she felt the first trickle of sweat across her forehead. 'I won't be needing to be in here for that long. I just wanted to ask you and your husband some questions about the death of his father. Did your father have any enemies?'

Alexei turned away at first, then back to look at Hope before Karina responded. 'His father was a very important man. Ruling Zupci, a new kingdom with a lot to do. It's put Alexei under a lot of pressure as well. Did he have enemies? Yes, but none of them are here. The people here love him,' said Karina.

Hope thought she was giving a speech, like a party broadcast, as opposed to a heartfelt assessment.

'Obviously, you're deeply troubled,' said Hope to Alexei. 'What was your father's fortune made in?'

'The Duke had business interests in a lot of areas,' said Karina. 'And Alexei has been running many of those for him. It's taken a heavy toll and with the death of his father, he's not really up to many questions.'

'What sort of business was he involved in, though?' asked Hope.

'Most of it is trade. Obviously, you can see we deal in antiquities as well. There are many items in the Zupci fortune.'

'I'm very impressed. The other sergeant, she used to work in the art world, and is very knowledgeable in these things. She's done nothing but rave on about the various items around the house. You say he's got no enemies here. Clearly, he had one. Do you have any suspicions about who may have done this?' Again, Hope directed the question to Alexei, but Karina answered.

'The only person we're unsure of is that instructor, the sports girl. The Duke took quite an interest in her. Pavel does too.

55

Maybe he took too much of an interest. Maybe she didn't like that. She's the only one I can think of. She would have been alone as well at night. Didn't have a boyfriend or anyone with her.'

'Were you alone that night?' asked Hope directly to Karina.

'Of course not. Alexei and I were in bed. I assume that the Duke was killed during the night. That's what sources have said.'

'Sources,' said Hope, 'which sources?'

'You don't believe we have an empire like this without having a few sources of our own. The report from Miss Nakamura indicated that the Duke was stabbed during the night. Is that correct?'

Hope didn't see the point in denying it, and besides, the sweat was now pouring down the side of her face. She could feel her jeans sticking to her.

'Maybe you and I should continue this conversation outside,' Karina said to her.

Hope shook her head. If needs be she'd go outside, strip off and get a towel and come back in because she wanted to see Alexei's face.

'Have you ever handled a weapon like the blade with which your father was stabbed?' asked Hope. 'Ever handled a weapon that could do that sort of damage?'

'What sort of a question is that?' asked Karina.

'Just the standard,' said Hope. 'We're trying to rule Alexei out of the equation. I'm not bringing him into it. That's already been done by simply being here.'

'You limeys have such a funny way of running things. You don't even have a gun on you, do you? You don't get that back in America.'

'I'm sure your American police force do things rightly, but here we run things our way. Alexei, tell me what happens with your business when your father dies. Who takes over?'

Again, Karina butted in for him. 'The thing is that . . . '

'Stop,' said Hope, very bluntly and with her hands held up. 'I'd like Alexei to answer. So far, he has answered nothing, and you've interjected each time. I'm not going to be sitting here for that much longer. So please, Alexei, who takes over now that your father's dead?'

The man looked up and began to stammer. 'There are a number of assets. Different people will take over. I will probably be in charge for them. I have overall control with people who work for me. It's a big business, a big family, lots to do.'

'He's well capable of it,' said Karina. Hope thought that her statement compared to his performance gave the most contrasting opinions that she'd ever faced.

'Is your mother happy that you've taken over?' asked Hope.

'It's the way,' said Karina. 'The male always inherits. It will go to Alexei, then it will go down to Victor, and then Pavel. Oh, dear God, let's hope it doesn't go to Pavel. Victor would probably squander it as well. But Alexei here, he has been groomed by his father for this. He's ready for it, aren't you, dear?'

Alexei put his hand up to his wife and accepted a kiss from her. 'We are,' he said. 'We are.'

'You still haven't answered my question,' said Hope. 'I asked about you holding a weapon, a knife. I asked if you'd handled a weapon like that before?'

'Never,' said Alexei.

'What about you, Karina?'

57

'Me neither.' As Hope sat sweating, she thought Alexei was telling the truth, but she had her doubts about Karina. It was too perfect an answer, too smooth. Alexei stuttered, but he seemed to think about the question.

'What about your guests that are with us?' asked Hope. 'Who invited them?'

'All invited by the Duke,' said Karina. 'Frank Schmidt has been a business contact for a long time. I'm not sure that Mischa was too keen on the two women that came. I don't know them very well.'

'What about you, Alexei?' asked Hope. 'Do you know any of the guests?'

'I've met Frank before in business dealings, also Lyla. Swen, too, and I knew Sarah, formerly.'

'What do you mean you knew her?' asked Hope.

'Well, it was before Karina.'

'Six months before me,' said Karina, her tone suddenly becoming quite firm.

'Sorry about that,' said Alexei. 'Sorry.'

'What do you mean sorry?' said Hope. 'I'm not following.'

Karina stood up holding her towel. She stepped down onto the floor of the sauna and asked Hope to step outside. With her t-shirt sticking to her like glue, and her jeans hugging her legs like a two-year-old child, Hope followed Karina out into the cooler air surrounding the swimming pool.

'He won't talk about that gold-digger.'

'How do you mean?' asked Hope.

'Sarah Kurtz, a former model. Well, it's not modelling, is it? I think you and I can speak as women and say it's just a form of prostitution, really, isn't it?'

'Can you clarify?' asked Hope.

'She was one of those models that showed everything in the magazines. The Duke was captured by her charms and so was Alexei, more recently. Six months before I met him, but he gave her up for me. Finally realised what a real woman looks like.'

'How did Sarah Kurtz feel about it?'

'How do you think she felt about it? Gold digger, money grabber. That's all she is. That's all she ever will be. Using everything she can to get there. I've turned him around; I'll tell you that. Alexei wouldn't be half the man he is today without me.'

Hope wondered what he was like before because the man didn't seem to talk.

'Do you accompany Alexei on the business trips?' asked Hope.

'It's the way we do it. I'm always there. It's a very old-school type of state. You go and you support your husband. You sit beside him. Of course you don't speak out formally. We haven't got that enlightened yet.'

'You're there for what? To be on show?'

'No, never. I wouldn't go for that,' said Karina. 'I'm there to support my husband in all things.'

'Is he always like this, though?' said Hope. 'Your husband seems incredibly agitated, very quiet.'

'It's the whole change of business that's going on, that's all. His father's just died, which in our work is enough to make any of us nervous, isn't it? If I was you, I would have a look at that sports instructor. Most of the rest of us are like family.'

'Even Sarah Kurtz?'

'Even Sarah Kurtz. That's why she's tolerated by me and Mischa.'

'Well, thank you for your time,' said Hope, and walked past the woman to reach down for a towel on the sun lounger. Hope hoisted her top up and gave herself a rub down, removing most of the sweat before replacing her top, deciding she needed to look for Macleod.

Alexei's reaction was bizarre. Was he falling apart because his father had died? Was he falling apart from the weight of what he would now have to take on? Hope wondered if the whole family was like this. Karina certainly wasn't. She seemed the strong one in the partnership. Maybe the brothers were all like Alexei.

Chapter 08

Clarissa Urquhart decided she would take the second brother and determined to find Victor. In some ways, she was enjoying this case, because as she walked around the house she saw art pieces, many of which she would struggle to see anywhere else. Each one was worth a small fortune, and she wondered what type of family this was.

As she wandered along the hall, she studied each painting until she came to one of a small landscape. Examining it more closely, Clarissa recognised the signature in the bottom right-hand corner of the painting. It was from the seventeenth century, very old and by a little-known Argentinian painter, but it was believed to have been lost some time ago. Clearly, that wasn't correct. She'd put the value of it as close to half a million, but more than that, she loved the artwork on it. For several minutes, she stood looking at it. Curious, she put her hand out and grabbed a passing manservant.

'Do you know when they got this?' she asked. The man looked at her.

'I asked, do you know when they got this?'

The man shook his head. Clarissa let him go but then saw Ivan at the far end of the corridor. She shouted him over.

'How can I help you, ma'am?' he asked politely.

'Do you know when the family acquired this painting?'

'I believe it was possibly six years ago.'

'Do you know where from?'

'I don't talk to the family about where they get such items from. That's handled by them alone.'

'It was seen in Peru eight years ago,' said Clarissa.

'You seem to be very knowledgeable on this subject,' said Ivan. 'More knowledgeable than I. I bow to your greater understanding.'

'And I bow to your straight face,' said Clarissa. It looked like the joke was lost on Ivan, or maybe he just was a great actor.

'I'm looking for Victor. I need to talk to him in regard to the investigation. Would you know where he is, Ivan?'

'I shall lead you to him, Detective Sergeant, but I warn you, you may not like what you see. He's having some recreational time.'

'Would it be better if I brought him out to somewhere else to talk to? I mean, is he alone?'

'He's not alone. His partner Jenna is with him. I shall go in first and see if it's okay.'

'No, Ivan, you won't. I'll just see him. Just direct me to where he is.'

Ivan nodded politely, took Clarissa along the corridor and up a flight of stairs before arriving at a door, knocking on it and opening it. He stood at the door and announced Detective Sergeant Clarissa Urquhart.

Clarissa bolted into the room, looking around for the man and saw him lying in an open shirt and pants on a long sofa. As she looked to her right, she saw a young redheaded woman only about five feet tall, simply wearing a long t-shirt. There were two women around the pool table. Clarissa wondered what they'd done with their clothes. As she turned to face Ivan, she heard loud music playing. It was a gyrating rhythm. She was sure that out of the ten words she heard at least six of them were swear words. Apparently, somebody's booty wanted something done with it. Turning back to Ivan, she saw him shrug his shoulders before closing the door.

'Can we turn the music down?' shouted Clarissa.

Victor seemed to be looking in her general direction and he waved her over to him. Clarissa walked over, reached down and shouted at him.

'Can you turn the music down?'

She was dressed in her usual shawl with tartan trousers beneath and Clarissa had never felt so out of place. She'd gone from wandering through a classy display of an art collection she would dream of to suddenly being in some teen fantasy. At least that's what she thought young male teens dreamt about.

She tried to get the man to understand about the music. He reached up, put two hands on her and began forcing a kiss onto her. Clarissa reacted by driving her hand under his chest, hitting him hard, causing him to fall back onto the chair. His eyes rolled and he laughed somewhat. Coming back up to her feet, she turned around. Seeing the two women by the pool table, she turned away from them and walked up to the young redhead.

'Kill the music,' she shouted. The girl's focus seemed somewhat sloppy. At the second time of asking the redhead turned away and walked over to a cabinet which she opened and pressed a button. The room went silent.

'Who did that?' asked Victor, lying on the sofa. 'We want the music. You,' he said, pointing to Clarissa. 'Show me that booty.'

Clarissa was caught in two minds. Was she deeply offended, or did she just find the whole thing completely hysterical? She found nothing sexy in the entire image, but she turned to the two girls at the pool table.

'Find some clothes quick, but stay here,' she said. The two looked at her, then looked over at Victor. He had tilted his head back with his eyes closed. Clarissa wasn't too sure if he had gone back to sleep.

'It's okay,' said the redhead.

Clarissa turned back to her. 'Are you Jenna, Victor's girl-friend?'

'That's right,' she said. 'Who are you coming in here? He won't be happy about this. Not when he comes round.'

'How many days is that going to take?' quipped Clarissa. 'Look at him. Look at you. What about those two women there? Are you happy about that?'

'I did choose them for him,' said Jenna. 'Who are you anyway? I mean, who dresses like that?'

Clarissa towered over the girl. 'Detective Sergeant Clarissa Urquhart dresses like this. Frankly, what are you doing?'

'Chill out, grandma,' said the girl. 'Can I put the music back on?'

'No, you can't,' said Clarissa, noting that the other two women had returned, although she thought they could do with a lot more clothing. 'I need to ask you questions regarding the death of the Duke of Zupci. I see his son is taking it rather badly.'

'Victor doesn't give a toss,' said Jenna. 'Victor's got all the money. Alexei's got to do all the work. Victor just hangs out. I mean, wouldn't you?'

'These two with him. They are . . .?'

'Pretty expensive, but worth it,' said the girl.

'Have they ever met the Duke?'

'No,' said Jenna. 'They came over with us. They haven't been anywhere else. They haven't even been out of this room. Slept with us the other night.'

'Is that two nights ago?'

Jenna nodded. Clarissa turned to walk over to the women. 'Can you confirm you were in the bed of these other two, two nights ago?'

The girls nodded.

'All night?' asked Clarissa. Again, there was another nod. 'Okay,' she said. 'You can go stand outside. I want to talk to Jenna and Victor alone.'

The women seemed wary of her and Clarissa could understand why. There was probably something illegal in what they were doing. Maybe they supplied whatever drugs Victor seemed to be on. She turned back to Jenna, then walked over to Victor. He was sitting on the long sofa, running a hand across his chest.

'Did you like the Duke?' asked Clarissa.

'Yes,' Jenna said. 'Met him once. Called me a pretty little thing.'

'What about Mischa? Have you ever met her?'

'I keep out of Mischa's way. She's not very keen on Victor. You see, Victor's too chilled. She likes all that art stuff out there; probably, you do too. People like that, stuck up their own arse.'

'Where are you from, Jenna?'

'Pontypool. I met Victor on a rave, and then he took me off to a better rave than that. I haven't looked back. I haven't been home since.'

'What's up with him? Is he distraught? Is he laying there in a stupor because he's had too many drugs?'

'Probably a mix of both,' said Jenna. 'He didn't take his father's death well. Yes, he's high as a kite. He tried to snog you; he must be.'

Clarissa ignored the offensive comment and watched as Victor started to rise. He managed to pull himself up to sit on a sofa before looking over at Clarissa. 'Love the trousers,' he said. He looked at her for a moment and then he fell back down. 'Where's the other ones?' he said.

'Just popped out. Be back in a minute,' said Jenna.

'Where's my music?'

'She stopped it,' said Jenna, pointing at Clarissa.

'I wanted to ask you some questions. I want to talk to you about your father's death,' said Clarissa.

The man hauled himself up again and his eyes wildly tried to focus as Jenna moved to his side. 'No good,' he said. 'He's gone.'

'Your father was stabbed to death. Are you aware of that?'

'Father's dead, I know. That's why we celebrate him.' He reached out with his arms, grabbing Jenna, pulling her close. Clarissa turned away as the two of them got more intimate than they should have been in front of another person.

'Just tell me,' she said. 'Were you in bed with Jenna two nights ago? Did you stay in your room? Did you ever leave?'

Victor rolled up to his feet, lurching past Clarissa. She saw Victor half stagger over to the same system that Jenna had switched off. The music started to blare out again, hurting Clarissa's ears. The man went to the pool table, put something on it and seemed to sniff it up his nose. Anywhere else Clarissa would have arrested him instantly, but here with what was going on, she wasn't quite sure what her jurisdiction was, or indeed, what she should do about it.

As she turned to the door, the two women came back in, but this time they were minus the clothes they had put on for her. One glowered down at Clarissa. The music had started, so time to work. They began such a gyration that Clarissa looked away. She couldn't have shaken her bottom like that even at an early age.

She turned around to find the sofa occupied again by Victor, along with Jenna, both of them in a state that wasn't something you did with a police audience. Clarissa was no prude but this was vulgar beyond belief. She walked to the door and opened it to find Ivan still outside.

'I thought I'd better stay here just in case you needed any assistance,' he said.

'Assistance?' said Clarissa. 'Do I not look like I can handle myself?'

'Indeed,' said Ivan. 'But Mr Victor, a few times he has tried to encourage ladies in a somewhat unfortunate endeavour.'

'He can try to encourage me in whatever endeavour he wants,' said Clarissa. 'I'll break his neck. Do you know where he gets his drugs from, Ivan?'

'I've told you I run the house. I don't ask the family where things come from. You'll help me by not asking that again. We don't keep our jobs well by proffering too much information about the family, if you understand my meaning. Unlike your detective inspector, I think you can be spoken with in a sensible fashion. We are both, how should we put it, middle management.'

Middle management, thought Clarissa. *If anybody else insults me today, I'm liable just to punch them.*

She turned back to Ivan. 'Middle management, if you will. People of the world, I would say. Although that's not one I want to get into.' She nodded at the door. 'How long have those girls been here?'

'They arrived with Mr Victor and Jenna, and I assume they'll disappear with him.'

'Where do they go when they're not with him?'

'As far as I'm aware they've always been with him. They stay in his room. They are paid employees.'

'Of course. Thank you for your help, Ivan. I think I'll catch up with the Inspector. Probably best he doesn't come back to interview Victor today. Is he ever in a condition to be interviewed?'

Ivan shook his head and turned away. 'If you'll excuse me, I have duties to attend to.'

Then the music inside the room suddenly got even louder. Clarissa could hear some whoops and shouts, ones that certainly showed everyone was having a good time. *How the other half lives*, she thought. *It's not a half I want to be part of.*

Chapter 09

Macleod waited in one of the drawing rooms, looking at the many portraits and elaborate art figures around him. He didn't feel there was taste to the way they were laid out, like they were just plunked one after another. Of course, Clarissa could give a better opinion on that, but to Macleod's mind, if you had something so truly magnificent, you would display each and every one in its own right. They did that at galleries, museums; you didn't find everything just dumped together in a corner or along one wall. It was always put together nicely.

'It's like they don't know the value of them, isn't it, sir?'

Macleod turned and smiled at Ross. 'That's it exactly, Ross. That's it. What it must be to have this much money.'

'Why are we here?' asked Ross. 'I mean, I know there's been a murder. I know we investigate murders, but why are we here? I know they asked for you, but this island, isn't it part of their country, so to speak? I know it's like a holiday house, but I thought they also set it up almost like an embassy.'

'Not really, but most of the people here will have diplomatic status. That's why it's very awkward ground we're on. I've been invited in, asked to work on the case. I'm still not exactly sure if I arrest them or what. I wanted to bring them back over to Barra, to put our regulations in force, work the way we work. Apparently, that's not happening. Whatever it is between the two countries, it's important enough that we just play ball.'

'Very good, sir,' said Ross, turning away again, walking over to one of the items. It was a statue of a ballerina in gold with various jewels along it.

'It's not good though, is it? Having things like this. I mean, many royal families, they open up places. You have courts and that where you can walk around and look at them. This isn't, this is all their little treasures shoved away in a house somewhere. It's not even in their country.'

'Well, I'm sure they've got something similar back at Zupci,' said Macleod.

'I was reading,' said Ross dropping into a whisper, 'that the takeover or the breakaway, it was funded by a lot of not-very-nice money. Not entirely sure how right and proper things were done.'

'Indeed,' said Macleod, 'that may be the case, but that's not our issue at the moment. You can't solve things like that. That's up to other people to deal with.'

'I know, sir, but I was just thinking then, what sort of people are we with?'

'Well, we'll soon find out. We're about to talk to the eldest amongst them.'

The door opened and Ivan, with a terribly serious face, walked in. 'Madam Zupci will receive you now. This way please, gentlemen.'

The man stood at the door until Macleod and Ross had exited through it. Then he quickly strode ahead of them, taking them around a couple of corners before opening the door into another drawing room. Considering the island was so small, the house was like a Tardis. Macleod noticed the designer carpet on the floor. There was a large crest on it that he'd seen around the house. It must have been the family's crest, but all the same, the work in making the carpet like that was impressive.

Before him in a chair was a small woman dressed in black with a veil across her face. Ivan walked ahead of Macleod, turned and announced the inspector and his colleague, and then introduced Madam Zupci to them. The old lady gave a wave of the hand and Ivan departed. As he did so, Mischa, dressed in black, arrived along with her daughter Kira, again in mourning attire. They flanked the old woman on either side, down on their knees beside the chair, each taking a hand. Each hand was adorned with several rings of which Macleod could not identify the cost. If Clarissa had been here, no doubt she would've told him.

'You'll have to forgive Mama for she's not got the best English. At her age, she doesn't recall words as quick.'

'She'll have to forgive my lack of her own language,' said Macleod. 'Would you be happy to translate for us?'

'Of course, Inspector. Otherwise, your interview with Mama would be kind of pointless.'

There was almost a sneer when she said it and Macleod was wondering just what Mischa was. She had invited them in and for most people who wanted Macleod there, they generally showed a type of respect to him. It was almost as if she toyed with him.

Mischa broke into some Russian before turning to Macleod. 'She says she's ready. I've told her who you are, why you're here, so please ask away.'

Macleod felt very overbearing standing up in the middle of the floor, but as he hadn't been offered a seat, he continued to stand with Ross behind his shoulder.

'First of all, let me pass on my condolences on the death of your son. I intend to find out who did it. Quite what happens after that, I don't know, given the rather muddied jurisdiction we seem to be standing in. However, that won't stop me from identifying the killer. You have my word on that.'

The old woman reached forward slowly and croaked something into Mischa's ear.

'She thanks you for your service.'

Macleod gave up a polite nod, but he did wonder how much use this interview was going to be.

'Can I first ask, did your son have any enemies?'

Again, the woman leaned forward, whispering hoarsely into Mischa's ear. Mischa went to translate, but the woman kept talking and Macleod waited a full thirty seconds before the translation was forthcoming.

'She says the family has had enemies for a long time. People here, there, and everywhere, but now we're on an island—this is our sanctuary. The Duke had brought guests. Maybe the guests are the place to start.'

'If you'll forgive me,' said Macleod, 'I find a lot of the murders I deal with are family affairs. Things which have gone wrong internally. I walk around your house, and you have so much, money, status, wealth. You can even bend the will of my government at times. To be in charge of all of that would be quite the drive for any killer. Is there anyone within the family you would worry about who had a poor relationship with the Duke?'

72

The old woman sat back in the chair for a moment, and she reached round and took her veil, pulling it back. Macleod saw an old, wizened face. There were no teeth within the mouth, and she almost spat out a statement to him. He felt there was venom in it, anger, bitterness.

'She said we all have to be part of the family, and some take to it better than others.'

'That's all she said?' asked Macleod.

'That's the gist of it,' said Mischa.

'How did you feel about your son?' asked Macleod. 'Was he a good head of the family?'

The woman again kept the veil back off her face, but her head slumped this time. It was almost as if she babbled. With her head down, it made it hard to read her face, to see what sort of a comment she was making.

'That's a difficult question for Mama so forgive her for she's finding it difficult to talk about my husband.'

'For what reason?' asked Macleod.

'The reason her son is dead,' said Mischa, 'and so freshly. She just said, and indeed he always was, her pride and joy, the head of the family, the one guiding us on. You see, family is important for Mama. We're not like you, Inspector. We're not raised to follow our own careers. We were raised to be part of a strong family, a family that would make it, a family that would retain its rightful place. We'd been slighted for too long, and now here we are.'

'When you say back to take your rightful place, how exactly was that achieved?'

Macleod watched the old woman start to get up onto her feet. Mischa and Kira supported up under her arms, helping her. The old woman marched forward, stopped in front of

Macleod and looked into his face. She spat some words at him, then went to walk away.

'What did she say?'

Kira, this time turned around, quickly looking at Macleod with an angry pair of eyes.

'She said the staff don't get to ask those questions. You're here to find her son's killer; do your job.'

Macleod watched the three of them shuffle off, taking the old woman back out of the room. He thought on how poor an interview it had been. Yes, she was old, but she wasn't exactly cooperative. Maybe she was still in distress, he didn't know. As the three ladies reached the door, Mischa broke off, speaking some words to Kira before closing the door behind her and Yulia.

'Inspector,' said Mischa, coming back to Macleod, 'let me apologise for Mama. She suffered greatly these last couple of days. You have to understand; my husband was everything in her eyes. The hope for the family. We managed to get ourselves back in a place where we had the throne again, our own little part of the world, which may not seem like much to you, but when you have what you're owed, there is a feeling quite unlike any other. We were born to rule, you see.'

'Maybe you can answer this then,' said Macleod. 'You took back your kingdom. You got back to being in charge. How long ago was it the last time the family were in charge?'

'Hundreds of years. It's not a history you need to look into. The short version of how we got back in was tactically playing things politically well, and yes, a little bit of force. That much has to be admitted to. Then again, isn't that true of every revolution, every change of the wheel? Thankfully, in my husband, we had a man who did this, a man who could achieve.'

Macleod turned and looked around. 'You certainly have the money to be head of something such as this, and a confident head. I look around this island, I see servants downstairs, but what are they? Some sort of secret agents at the same time? I haven't seen a gun on any of them.'

'Back home, it's different,' said Mischa. 'Back home, we have to protect ourselves. There are still plenty of the dissidents within our little country, but here, here we are different. Here we are able to be ourselves amongst our kids. Yes, you are right, and very perceptive, Inspector. Some of our servants are not simply servants. That's why we brought them here. We established the house as an embassy of sorts so we have certain protections. It's a home away from home.'

'The one thing I've learned from today,' said Macleod, 'and I haven't learned a lot from my conversation, is that Madam Zupci is no threat. She certainly didn't kill your husband.'

'Perish the thought, Inspector. I believe that's how you put it. That was her son. She loved him. He was hers and she was immensely proud of him. Tell me, how is the case going? Have you checked over our sports instructor?'

'Julie McGeehan seems the most unlikely suspect going. One, you invited her. Two, she's never had any other contact with you at all. Of all the people in this island, she's about the least likely to have killed your husband. How did you find her? Did you pick her? Did your husband pick her to come?'

'She was available, and we hired her from a company. It wasn't anything unusual in that. It wasn't me who wanted her here. My husband likes the sports, and he thought that the guests would enjoy having her about to teach them how to do things properly. Some of our guests are into sports. I'm not a lover of exercise myself, but well, Julie looks after them.'

'It seems that your son, Pavel, has an interest in Julie.'

'Pavel has an interest in anything that moves with a pair of legs,' said Mischa suddenly. 'I wouldn't put too much stock in it. He's just at that age.'

'Well, I need to get on,' said Macleod. 'I've got plenty of other people to go and talk to, especially your guests.'

'Of course, Inspector. I shall leave and let you get on with it, but please, work fast. It's unsettling for the family not knowing what's going on.'

Macleod gave a nod as Mischa turned to leave the room, sweeping out of it with a very deliberate walk.

'I don't trust her, sir,' said Ross.

'She's certainly confident, really, and she's at the heart and soul of this family. I actually wonder what her husband was like.'

'He's not like they're telling you,' said Ross.

'Why? Your research come up with that? You should have said last night, Ross.'

'No, sir. My Russian isn't great, but they did not describe that man as the pride and joy of the family. Madam Zupci said nothing of the sort.'

'What did she say?'

'Best as I could make out, she said something about worm. It was wholly derogatory.'

'Yulia Zupci. Is she Mischa's mother?'

'No, she's the Duke's,' said Ross. 'The woman kept on describing him as a worm though.'

'That's very unusual for a mother unless he's really disappointed in some way. It would be good to know the man's history, I mean the real stuff, Ross, not just the headlines.'

'I don't have much on them, sir, not out with the family. Yes, he's seen them rise as they have come to take over the country. He's had dealings with lots of companies, but his personal history is very unclear. I guess the authorities in Zupci would be able to tell you, except they seem to tell us nothing.'

Macleod nodded. 'Makes you think though, doesn't it?'

'It makes you think what?'

'The old woman sitting here needing help. Mischa's there. Kira is there. The daughter is all in black. I haven't seen the older men showing her formality like that. I wonder if they've even been to see the old woman. Something about this family doesn't sit with me.'

The door opened after a knock and Ivan showed Hope into the room. Once the door had closed, she came over to Macleod.

'Apparently, there's clay pigeon shooting going on at the far side of the island with all the guests. It's certainly the strangest wake I've been to. I went to see the oldest son who was actually in trunks and he was sitting in a steam room. They don't seem too perturbed about what's happened.'

'No one does. I'll wait for Clarissa and then we'll make our way over to this clay pigeon shoot,' said Macleod. Once again, the door was knocked. Ivan opened it and Clarissa walked in. Macleod thought she looked rather hot and bothered. Once the door closed behind, he cocked his head to one side. 'Something up, Sergeant?' he asked.

'Next time, you take them. Next time, you talk to the second son. I've never seen debauchery like it.'

'Not in a sombre mood then,' said Macleod.

'Could we have a drink in here?' asked Clarissa. 'I could do with a stiff one.'

Macleod looked over. 'Sit down,' he said. 'Who's got you like that? I want to know about it.'

Chapter 10

When Macleod stepped outside, he didn't think it was the best day for a clay pigeon shoot. The wind was already picking up and the drizzle had turned into driving rain. He was taken with Hope by a servant across the island by buggy cart to the far end, where he saw a concrete shelter. Jenny McGeehan was standing in wet weather gear, welcoming some of the other guests.

Rather than turn up with a full team, Macleod had left Ross and Clarissa to continue in the house among the servants and find out any more about the family that they could. Meanwhile, Hope had joined him, hoping to find more out about the guests that have been invited to the island. Leaving the buggy, Macleod quickly ran inside the concrete shelter and almost bumped into a strong, tall individual.

'Excuse me,' said Macleod. 'Just wanted to get in out of the rain. Who might you be?' Macleod knew who it was. There was no mistaking the large Swede, Swen.

'I am Swen Drummond and we are here to shoot, so I hope you won't get in the way, Inspector.'

'There's no need for that,' said Macleod. 'I'm sure my colleague would enjoy some shooting.'

'If Mr. Drummond's up for it,' said Hope, and she saw the man smile briefly before turning away. She leaned over into Macleod's ear. 'You know I don't do guns. I can't stand them.'

'Get close, find out. You have to play this differently. Mix in. They're going to want to talk to you more than they'll want to talk to me.'

'Such an honour,' whispered Hope before she turned away and followed Swen Drummond to the far corner where guns were being issued.

'What about yourself, Inspector?' Jenny McGeehan asked.

'I'm fine,' he said. 'How many of the others here are shooting?'

'I think we all are, Inspector.'

'Feel free to call me Seoras since we're out in a little party,' said Macleod, forcing himself to sound jolly. This was out of his comfort zone. He was used to going into places dictating how he'd react, who would say what, putting people under pressure. Right now, he was the one feeling under pressure.

'Frank,' said the man. 'Frank Schmidt.' He was closer to Macleod's height and also to his age.

'You're a business partner with the Zupcis, I believe.'

'Had many dealings for a long time. Small nation like that, you need to work with people on the outside as well. Keep everything to a mutual benefit. That's what I say.'

'So, you knew the Duke for a while?' said Macleod.

'Ever the Inspector, aye?'

'Seoras. Call me Seoras today.' It was a pretty weak attempt by Macleod to try and generate a different atmosphere and less suspicion about himself. A poor attempt he was only too aware of.

'You always seem a little bit pricklier on the screen,' said a female voice. Macleod turned to see Lyla Preen, the former actress.

'I'm not sure I've caught many of your films,' said Macleod, 'but I'm told you're quite the actress.'

'And I'm told you're quite the detective. Although whenever I've seen you on the television, you have been a lot more formal. Nice to know the man behind it.'

'Well, not many people get to see this side of me,' said Macleod. 'I was told that the Duke backed some of your films; is that correct?'

'That's true, although I did fall a little bit out of favour. Although I don't think that was the Duke that did that.'

'How do you mean?' asked Macleod.

'Well, I'm still here, aren't I? Mischa always thought she had control over him, but he had tastes beyond the brunette.'

'Forgive me for asking you something,' said Macleod, 'but was this taste still continuing here?'

'You're asking me to kiss and tell, Inspector. I'm afraid that's not something I'll do.'

'Did Mischa know?' asked Macleod, trying to feign innocence.

'Well, I knew,' said Frank. 'And if I knew, I guess Mischa must have. This might be a different world to what you're used to working in.'

'Well, I'm used to dealing with bodies,' said Macleod. 'People who are angry with each other. People who don't trust each other. Jealousy, hatred, business connections gone wrong. I think I've seen my fair share to know people.'

There was a slight kerfuffle outside, before a woman entered in an outfit that would've been better suited to poolside.

'Aha, the inspector,' said the woman, looking at Macleod. He did his best to turn his attention away from the bare legs that were walking into the room.

'Sarah Kurtz, I presume,' said Macleod. 'Pleasure to meet you.'

'Of course, it is.'

The woman strolled in as if she was the centre of the room and Macleod could see the photographic qualities about her that had made her a star. Shame, he thought, that she had to go to the type of photography that let everybody know everything, because he thought she could have made it easily enough as some sort of catwalk model. Macleod wasn't against fashion, but he was against the over-exploitation of the female body.

'If everyone will remain in here, stepping back, we've got the pod areas at the front where we'll shoot from, and I believe Mr Drummond and Sergeant McGrath are ready to shoot.'

'It's just Hope today,' said McGrath from the other side of the room.

'I can see why you kept her on your team,' said Frank, nudging Macleod.

'I think you'll find, Mr Schmidt, that Hope's on my team because she can size people up and get to the bottom of what they're about.'

'She's a cracking bird, though, isn't she? Pity about that scar across her face.'

Macleod could feel his fist clench. The scar had come from Hope saving Macleod's partner. The reminder brought back Jane's current state, too. Macleod was angry he was having to deal with this circus rather than being with her, but more to the point, Frank was being rude about his colleague.

'I wouldn't try anything with Hope, Frank,' said Macleod. 'She sees through people for what they want. She's also wholly professional.'

'You think she'd come and be my security consultant?'

'No,' said Macleod, rather too quickly and too abruptly.

'Can't blame a man for trying, though. Maybe I will try.'

Macleod was feeling more and more uncomfortable in this environment, but he watched as a cry of, 'Pull,' was heard. Swen Drummond had the double-barrelled gun in his hands and Macleod saw two clay pigeons blown to smithereens.

Ten seconds later, there was another cry of, 'Pull,' and he watched as Hope clipped one before missing the other completely.

'I thought you guys would be good with guns,' said Lyla Preen.

'We don't carry guns generally in the Scottish police force. We don't use them unless we have to. I use my mind to solve cases, not my muscles.'

Sarah now walked over to take up a gun and stand in one of the pods, ready to call. Frank leaned close into Macleod again.

'Look at that,' he said. 'She won't be able to handle the gun, of course, but she'll like being up in front of everybody. That sort of woman.'

Macleod ignored him, but then thought better of it. 'Sarah used to be heavily involved with the Duke?'

'Oh, yes,' said Frank. 'The Duke was after that one big time. I mean, they were banging.'

'When was this?' asked Macleod, forcing himself to ignore the crassness.

'All through when they were coming to power, all the way up. She was his fancy woman. At first, he kept her in a house here, there, wherever, but then I thought he made a mistake. He brought her in, into the palace, back in Zupci. I remember

83

being over visiting him, doing some business dealings and lo and behold, out popped Sarah. I mean, fine by me. She's never been a disappointment to my eyes, but Mischa was rattled. There's an expression, isn't there? You don't shit on your own doorstep. That's how you Brits put it, isn't it?'

'You don't cheat on your wife, is how I would put it,' said Macleod, 'but your rather vulgar take on it is pretty accurate.'

Frank laughed. 'You need to lighten up. Policemen in Zupci are much lighter, easier to deal with, but I guess you're never off duty, are you? Come on, have a drink.'

Macleod turned and saw champagne had been brought out.

'I don't. I never have. Part of the world I come from, it was greatly shunned, and I've shunned it ever since, but please don't let me stop you.'

Macleod nearly jumped after he heard the call of, 'Pull,' and two more gunshots were loosed off. However, two clay pigeons had escaped and Sarah Kurtz gave a little laugh.

Small canapes were brought out as the shooting continued, with both Frank and Lyla now getting involved, and the conversation started to flow around what had happened. Macleod noted that everyone was speaking reasonably freely, except for Swen. Macleod waited until the man had taken up the gun again and was shooting another round before turning to Frank.

'What's the deal with Swen then? He doesn't say much, does he?'

'I thought you would've clocked him pretty quickly.'

'Who says I haven't? Maybe I'm looking for your opinion.'

'You're looking for my opinion about a hitman?' queried Frank. Macleod gave a little look of shock across his face. 'Oh, he's good,' said Frank. 'That's probably why you don't know him. I dare say the Duke's used him plenty as well. Can't be too careful in this business if you know what I mean.'

'In what way do you mean that?'

'You do realise who you're dealing with here,' said Frank. 'The Zupcis. They've risen to power and that, but you don't mess with them.'

Macleod looked at the man and saw that he was staggering slightly more than he had at the beginning of the session. Macleod had watched him put plenty of champagne away, followed by some whisky and maybe the man was now more inebriated than he should have been.

'Business with them hasn't always been easy. I mean, I realise you're a police officer, but you're not here officially; that's what Mischa said. With the Zupcis, there's been times when I've had a few boys feel the sharp end of their anger. You've got to deal with them in a good way. Got to make sure everything goes smoothly. They're well worth dealing with and they have plenty of money pass through them and with them, but get it wrong and they snap hard. Kind of a family tradition. I don't think I'll say much more about that.'

'Your turn, Frank,' said Julie McGeehan. Macleod watched Frank stagger forward to pick up a gun. Fortunately, Julie was there to make sure he was pointing it in the right direction. One thing Macleod was surprised about was the guests were getting guns, considering what had happened, but then again, there were so many people about, to actually kill anyone would've given you away as the murderer pretty quickly. As Macleod stood holding a cola in his hand, Lyla Preen edged up beside him.

'Did they buy you to be here?'

'What makes you say that?' asked Macleod.

'They can buy everyone, can't they? They bought me with the films. I was promised a whole film series, movie after movie, by the Duke. Of course, he wanted certain things in return, but that was worth it until she pulled the plug.'

'Mischa?' asked Macleod.

'No, Yulia. You watch where power comes from in the family. They have that expression, don't they, foreigners. The men, they're the head of the family, but the women, they're the neck. They're making them turn. Look where they want to look. They're guiding them, steering them, real captains of the ship. If it hadn't been for her, I'd have been a bigger movie star than I already am.'

Macleod couldn't remember seeing many of her movies. From Ross's briefing, he remembered that they were rather full on.

'How does it feel doing movies like that?' asked Macleod. 'Did you never want to be like a Shakespearean actress or something?'

'Shakespearean actresses are not famous, are they? Think about it. Royal Shakespeare Company. Who's in it at the moment? Who's there doing this or that? Nobody you know. You only know them when they go and do the other roles and then they tell you they were RSC. You do these movies so everybody knows your name. You do what you have to do to get there. The Duke gave me a way in.'

'Well, if you were on your way out, why are you back here?'

'You see, Seoras—by the way, that's a cute name—the thing is the Duke looked at me for other reasons. The movies were just what he threw at me to get me to go along with him. He still wanted to have his cake and eat it.'

'I'm assuming he got his way, as you're here,' said Macleod.

'How did the family feel about that?'

'The family?' blurted Lyla in a loud voice before dropping back down. 'Have you seen their family? One wonders how they ever made it. Don't get me wrong, Seoras, I might do things that you might not agree with and you might think I show too much of myself to the world, but I'm in charge with what I do. I choose to do it. This family, a lot of them are just all over the place. The Duke was one of them. He just wanted to enjoy life. He wanted to throw that money around and take what he wanted. I was just lucky enough to be on the list.'

Lyla marched off to grab another bottle of champagne. Macleod looked over to see Hope walking towards him. 'Starting to get the hang of it, Seoras,' she said. 'Not getting much out of Swen, though.'

'No, you're not, are you? Quiet man.'

'He can shoot, though,' said Hope. 'I mean really shoot. I'm not sure he's missed one yet. I'll tell you something else.'

'What?'

'Eyes everywhere. He hasn't taken more than two moments to shoot before he's looking back to see who's talking to who and what's going on.'

'What are you thinking?' asked Macleod.

'I'm thinking he's working for someone. Question is who. What did you find out?' she asked quietly.

'Dysfunctional family with friends that have had the rug pulled out from under their feet at times, now back in the fold. Nobody seems to be a friend with the whole family.'

'So, we're narrowing down the suspects really well, then,' laughed Hope.

'Rogues' gallery,' said Macleod. 'We were right last night. It's all a rogues' gallery.'

Chapter 11

'Looks like we're in luck, sir,' said Ross as he pointed out to the clouds surrounding the island. 'They don't look too bad. I mean, the sea's quite choppy, but we'll get back.'

'We will, but what worries me about the next couple of days, will we be able to get back over here, to Mingulay?'

'Do you feel like we've gotten anywhere?' asked Hope.

Macleod turned and looked at her and gave a quick shake of his head. 'Feelings, ideas, superstitions, who knows? Thoughts like that,' said Macleod. 'Nothing concrete, nothing definite.'

'Well, it couldn't have been anything concrete or definite. Killed in the middle of the night. Everybody saying, 'I'm in my room.' Some with other people. Looks like a big stitch up to me,' said Clarissa.

'That's not exactly helpful, is it?' Macleod muttered back.

'I suppose not, Seoras. Come on quick, so we catch this boat.'

Several servants carried the few bags that Macleod and Hope had with them. Jona had returned from the island some time ago and in truth, Macleod was looking forward to getting into Barra, putting his feet up in the hotel and placing a call to Jane. He wasn't sure how she was doing. When he contacted her previously, she was on the defensive because he was working, and she never wanted to burden him when he was working. *At least Angus was there*, he thought. *At least someone was there if she fell apart.*

No, it should have been him. What was he doing in this comic situation? *Comic*, he thought. *What a choice of words. There's a man dead. There's a man dead and yet they all behave as if life just goes on, as if this is normal.*

Maybe it is where they came from. Were they a bunch of criminals? Is that what it was? Cutthroat ones at that. Who would keep these guests around them, despite the fact there was a killer there? Knife wounds into the chest, not from below, from above or at least on the level. He mused as he got into the boat, sat down in the aft section and watched the captain come through from the wheelhouse.

'Inspector Macleod, are you ready to go? I think we should get a shift on. It's not meant to be good through the night.'

'Whenever you're ready. I think we're all aboard.'

The captain returned to the wheelhouse, started the engine and Macleod watched as the boat gently moved away from the pier. As it did so, he saw in the distance someone running down from the house. He wasn't quite sure, but it may have been Ivan. The man looked puffed, as if he couldn't run that distance, but had to, was compelled to.

'Captain, could you just hold up for a minute?'

'Aye. What's the problem, Inspector?'

'There's somebody coming down towards the pier at full pelt, probably wants to talk to us. Can you take her back in?'

'Of course, I can. But like I said, we don't want to be here too long or it's going to be an overnight stay.'

'That's understood,' said Macleod and stepped off the boat

back onto the pier as the captain brought it alongside.

'Inspector,' shouted Ivan to him from a distance. It was unlike the man. He was normally cool and calm, giving the idea of being in overall charge and yet, here he was almost flapping. 'Inspector. We need you. We need you now.'

'Why?' asked Macleod. 'What's gone wrong?'

'It's Victor, sir. Master Victor's been killed.'

Macleod turned to the boat and waved at the team. 'Hope, Clarissa, back out, bring your stuff. Ross, take the boat back to Barra. We might need to bring you over in the morning. I'll let you know.'

'I'll let Angus know what's happened. He can . . . '

'Of course,' said Macleod, thanking Ross for bringing up something that was going to slip his mind. He'd reached a relative state of calm, getting on the boat, waiting for that small journey back over to Barra and he was going to have an evening's rest. He'd speak to Jane, and he'd put his feet up, maybe even have a bath. Now, all of a sudden, the maelstrom had started again. He reached down, giving a hand to Clarissa and pulling her out of the boat. She plopped her bag down beside him and Hope took Macleod's out on her own, placing them all together.

'Ivan, when you get a chance, you come down, you pick up these bags, and you take them to the house. Now, where are we going?'

Ivan nodded profusely, began to run towards the house, and then went into a brisk walk instead.

'No need for the hurry, is there?' said Clarissa behind Macleod. 'I mean, if he's dead, he's dead. They don't get any better after that.'

'Not confirmed dead. Hope, go.' Hope turned and gave

Macleod a nod. Of the three of them she was easily the fittest and would be quickest in getting there. She tore off ahead of Ivan, who briefly tried to break into a run again and follow her but failed miserably.

'He's more my pace,' said Clarissa.

Just as they reached the house, the rain began to fall. Macleod stopped briefly at the door, looked around and seeing a Hebridean scene he knew all too well, one Ross has missed. The storm was coming in. No wonder the captain wanted to get that boat back. It would be a problem. In three hours' time, it would be a real problem. Then Macleod remembered the bags. Stepping inside the house, Ivan brushed past him, indicating that he should go this way, but Macleod stopped the man.

'Send someone for the bags now.'

Ivan gave a start, then turned and shouted in Russian to a young lad who looked miserable at the idea that he was about to step out into the pouring rain. Ivan led Macleod down a corridor, up several flights of stairs, and across a landing before Macleod saw the open door and a couple of staff standing outside. One young girl was weeping bitterly while another had her arm around her. There were none of the family to be seen, which surprised Macleod. As he got to the door, he saw a large bedroom.

'This is Victor's chambers?' asked Macleod. Ivan nodded. 'Where are you, McGrath?'

'In here, Inspector.' Macleod looked over at a door that was open on the far side of the room. He made his way past the four-poster bed and the large colour TV on the wall with the enormous sound system. He saw a couple of other doors, presuming they were walk-in wardrobes of some sort, and instead followed Hope's voice and saw she was in a large bathroom.

To say bathroom was an understatement in the extreme. Sure, there was a toilet, wash-hand basins and a rather gaudy-looking, gold-edged mirror, but what dominated the room was the large Jacuzzi. The room was filled with steam at the moment, condensation dripping off the walls and obscuring the mirror, and the Jacuzzi was still bubbling away. Sprawled across one side of it were two naked women, neither moving, their heads hanging backwards and mouths open. Jenna was lying face down in the water, half of her sprawled across Victor. His head seemed twisted, his neck in an unusual angle. Macleod stepped closer.

'Back, sir. I'm just wanting to make sure we're isolated here. There's something in that water.'

'Something in the water? Like what?'

'Like a large stereo system.'

Macleod glanced at the far side of the Jacuzzi and could see the wire running into the pool. He watched as Hope traced it back. It ran through a small room into which she disappeared.

'It's just like a broom cupboard of some sort. Small. I don't know what they kept in here. Hang on, I've got the plug. I'm going to pull it out.' Hope appeared in the bathroom a few seconds later, holding the plug in a latex-gloved hand.

'Just in case,' she said. 'Should be safe now.'

Macleod stepped closer. 'Somebody, turn the Jacuzzi off,' he said. 'It's going to take a while for Jona to get here and if she does, I don't want her coming to a load of poached lobsters.' Macleod saw Ivan raise his eyes at him but he turned instead to the man. 'Does Madam Zupci know?'

'I sent someone to tell her. My first thought was to come

and get you. But she should do.'

'We might want to make sure about that. She's not here, after all. In fact, no one from the family's here.'

'It's literally just happened, sir.'

Macleod turned round to Clarissa who'd followed them into the room. She was sweating, standing inside the steamed bathroom with her shawl wrapped round her.

'Clarissa, find out where everyone is. Find out where they've been for the last twenty minutes. Don't let anyone come out of their rooms; ask them to stay there.'

'Mischa's not going to like that, is she?'

'I don't care what she likes or not. Her son's dead. Her husband's dead. What is this? If they want me to run a murder investigation, I need some leeway to run it. Go before we lose them.'

'That's a lot of ground to cover on her own, Seoras.' Hope was checking the pulse of the silent figures in the Jacuzzi, and shook her head to communicate the result.

'You're right. Go, Hope. Give her a hand.' Macleod then turned to Ivan. 'Everyone stays outside of this bedroom and this bathroom. No one comes in. You go to the door, and you ensure that. I'm tasking you with this and if it goes wrong, I'm coming for you. Your mistress has given me authority to run an investigation.'

'I understand. It will be done.'

Macleod watched the man disappear back out and he wasn't quite sure how he felt about him. He certainly seemed suspicious of Macleod at times, but then again, he seemed suspicious of everyone. Maybe he was the protection here in the house. Were they really servants or somebody's closer protection? Macleod turned back to the scene in front of him.

Macleod wasn't unused to debauchery, although he did abhor it. If Victor had been there with simply just Jenna, he wouldn't have batted an eyelid, but it was the other two women that were there. Clarissa had said they were women of the night. He knew that was a dig at him when she'd said it. Such an old-fashioned term, polite and yet packed with meaning and disdain for those it was referring to.

He moved closer, trying to cast his detective eye around the scene. He wondered if Jona looked at these bodies, how many would be filled with drugs? He could see none on the poolside but when he glanced over to the sinks, he saw thin white lines of powder. He knew what type of drug it was, expensive powder you sniff up your nose which certainly wouldn't be good for you. Someone had walked in and dropped the sound system in. You wouldn't have electrics in the bathroom like this. Apparently, Victor hadn't minded.

Macleod heard a kerfuffle at the door to the bedroom, and he turned and marched his way across the bedroom towards it. He saw Mischa standing at the door with Ivan, blocking her away.

'It's okay, Ivan, you can let her into here.'

Mischa began to march across the bedroom floor, but Macleod put his hand out. 'Stop.'

She looked at him fiercely. 'My son is in there.'

'He is indeed,' said Macleod. 'I'm sorry for your loss, but that's a crime scene. You can't just march in. We've secured it. Now I need everybody to stay out of it.'

'I need to see him. I need to see my boy.'

Tears were streaming down the woman's face, her hair distraught as she stood wrapped up in a black silk dressing gown.

'Slowly with me,' said Macleod. He took her by the hand, walking her gently over towards the door. He watched her face as she looked in, saw the horror creep across it.

'Somebody threw the sound system into the Jacuzzi. Looks like they've all been electrocuted. We've checked and there's no pulse.' Macleod watched Mischa carefully and caught an arm around her as she tried to race forward into the bathroom. 'No,' he said. 'No, no, no, we don't do that. We're not doing that.'

'I need to see him.'

'No, you don't. He's gone.'

There was more commotion at the door of the bedroom, and Macleod saw Ivan holding back Pavel and Alexei. He then heard Clarissa ordering them back to their room. The scene was a mess. As he stood with Mischa crying into his shoulder, he wondered what to make of it all. He needed to get a hold of Ross, get Jona over, and see what had happened. He wasn't quite sure how it would work if they had to leave the bodies like this for a day or two. They were sitting in warm water, not an ideal crime scene.

Macleod turned with Mischa, taking her back towards the door and was surprised to see Swen standing at it, looking in.

'I believe my sergeants would've asked you to return to your room,' said Macleod. Swen looked past him regardless, and then Macleod saw him cast his eye at Mischa. She continued to cry, leaning on him for support.

'I said back to your room, sir. I've kind of got my hands full at the moment, but we're going to speak to you soon.'

Swen gave a curt nod, turned on his heel and walked off. Macleod passed Mischa over to Ivan.

'See that your mistress gets back to her room. We'll be up to speak to you soon. Madam, again, I'm sorry for your loss.'

Standing in the hallway outside the door to the bedroom, Macleod watched as a number of servants continued to hang around the doorway. He felt as if he was being watched, but being the only one there, he had to make sure that the room was guarded and not interfered with. He would let his sergeants go get the information, see if there was any way of identifying who could have been down here. But something about it was bothering him. Like the first murder, he reckoned nobody would have an alibi except possibly for their loved ones, for those closest to them. Considering the suspects, that wasn't an alibi worth anything.

Then that question came back to him. What was he doing here? What were they doing here? Why wouldn't they solve this on their own? He didn't take the fame and fortune line. Oh, Macleod is this, Macleod is that.

Looking out at the corridor, a crowd, half with weeping faces and the rest looking sullen, he wondered if any of them knew. And Mischa, the crying mother. He wasn't quite sure what to believe there, but he did know he wasn't getting back to Barra anytime soon.

Chapter 12

I t was in the early morning by the time that Macleod and the team had satisfied themselves that the crime scene was going to remain secure, although Macleod wasn't sure if it'd ever truly be secure. The door had been locked off at the bedroom and at all other access points with the keys given to Clarissa to hold. Copious photographs had been taken by Hope of the entire area for Jona was unable to come back across. The weather had worsened significantly and there was no chance of the boat returning.

On the advice of Jona, the Jacuzzi had been drained of its water and the bodies left in as best a condition as they could be before being covered over. It was all very makeshift and not ideal, but as Macleod had said to Hope, 'This is anything but a normal investigation.' It was four in the morning as Hope stood in the room she'd been given, looking out to the edges of the island. The rain was beating down hard, and the wind having whipped up while the seas looked as rough as anything through the occasional splash of moonlight that the rolling clouds allowed.

She had followed Macleod to many crime scenes, but this one felt very different. She envied Ross. *Happy, back in the hotel room. He was probably fast asleep by now.* Who was she kidding? He'd be up on that blasted computer working away trying to make a difference to the investigation, looking for some seed that was hidden deep. It wouldn't be the first time he'd found one. A sliver of information that blew a case wide open.

Hope stepped into her own en suite bathroom, but it didn't have a large Jacuzzi inside; instead, it was a simple shower unit and she stripped off, turned the water on so it was hot, and let herself stand underneath. She thought of John, her man, back at the flat in Inverness and realised this was one of the things she was beginning to hate about detective work. If the cases were around Inverness, it was usually okay because she could drive to him each day, but something like this on the islands, then she was away from him for a while. Maybe that was a good thing. Maybe it was confirming how serious she was about him. He certainly seemed to be serious about her.

Stepping out of the shower, she dried herself down before slipping into a pair of bedroom shorts and T-shirt. She wasn't one for wearing much in bed, but she also felt when she was away on her own, it was probably best these days to have something on in case she had to get out of bed quickly. Macleod would've laughed at her for that, but she was being practical.

Hope lay down in the bed provided, which was large, something that bothered her. She didn't mind large beds if somebody was in there with her, but when you were on your own, it just reminded you that they weren't with you. She rolled over several times before getting up and walking over to the window of the room. She left the light off, pulled the curtains back, and looked out.

There was somebody downstairs. She peered down, seeing the person close one of the doors and step out into the rain. Wearing tight, black clothing, possibly rainproof, in the poor light there was, it looked like a male figure. She didn't know who it was.

At this hour of the morning, this isn't right. Spinning round she dropped her shorts, grabbed a pair of track bottoms, and pulled them on. She wrapped her coat around her, forced her feet into her trainers, and walked quickly through the floors of the house. Although there were lights on, everywhere was quiet, and Hope made sure that she didn't create any noise, creeping along quietly but quickly.

When she reached the door the man had come out of, she opened it slowly and scanned around her, but there was no one lurking outside. She stepped out, closing the door behind her and held her position, looking around. She clocked a figure in the distance walking slowly over towards one of the storehouses for the outdoor equipment. She had seen the building when she was interviewing Jenny McGeehan but hadn't been inside.

As soon as Hope stepped beyond the lee of a side wall, she felt the rain bite into her face. If it hadn't been for the jacket, she'd have been soaked almost instantly, but her track bottoms became wet and clung to her as the wind blew hard. Her legs felt cold and her red hair whipped around her because she'd stepped out without tying it up.

Hope ignored the cold around her knees and crept out towards the store, arriving at the side door, but the figure had gone in. She raced around the outside trying to look in through a couple of windows, cautiously peering, but it was too dark to see. There was a rear door and slowly she opened it, praying it wouldn't make a sound. To the outside, any sound would be lost in the wind, but to the inside, she wasn't so sure.

When the door was half opened, she crept inside, closing it gently and then dropping down to her knees. The room was full of coasteering equipment as well as other abseiling and climbing gear. Through an open door, she could see kayaks in the other store. Whoever it was creeping about was in there for she could hear movement.

Hope held her ground initially before moving off to one side, hiding behind a large drum. She didn't know what was inside the storage item and she didn't look, instead, peering around it trying to catch a glimpse of whoever was in the other room. She didn't have to wait long before the shadowy figure came through. Hope leaned back in behind the drum.

Hope felt her nerves on edge as the person came closer and she gripped her hands together into a fist, ready to stand and fight if she had to. Of course, there could be a perfectly rational explanation why someone would be out here in the dark wandering around in the early hours of the morning. No, there wasn't. If she interrupted them, the high likelihood is they would either flee or attack, and given that you couldn't flee very far in this island, attack would probably be the main option.

She heard the figure move away to the other side of the store she was in, but Hope kept her ground, hoping to catch a glimpse. As she did so in the dark, she was able to ascertain the frame of the man, for it was definitely a man. The shoulders were not feminine; the hips certainly weren't.

She watched as he searched a desktop beside the window. A glimpse of moonlight splashed his face for an instant, but it was all that Hope needed. It was Swen and this cut her to the core. A hit man stealing around, on the hunt for something. She certainly didn't want to surprise him in case he reacted in a violent manner. Better to observe, better to . . . She pulled her head back in behind the barrel.

Footsteps came closer, and then Swen opened the door that Hope had come in by. After a few moments, she made her way to the window to see if she could spot the man's next move. She caught a glimpse of him as he headed off around the rear of the house. Quickly, Hope opened the door and followed him, clinging close to buildings. She watched him walk around the edge of a tennis court before making his way into another small shed. In the driving rain and the cold dark, Hope raced after him.

As she got close to the shed, she realised that there were no windows. She tried to listen in through the walls. The only thing she heard was the door of the shed opening again. The door was to her right side, so Hope ran left and stood behind the shed listening carefully, standing out of the wind in the lee of the shed. She heard a crunch as Swen walked around the edge of the store. He was coming on the path where she was, so she continued going round the shed until she came to the door and entered.

Swen was outside, but what bothered her was he had circled the shed. Did he know someone was there? Once inside, she struggled to see and hit her foot on something metal. She bit her tongue in a desperate bid not to cry out but continued to feel her way into the shed. She rolled down underneath some shelving, tucking herself in tight.

The door opened again, but she could just about make out a pair of feet entering until the door was shut and the light came on. He was clearly looking for something as he began to scan the shelves. Hope tried her best to pull herself back in as hard as she could underneath the shelving.

Control your breathing, Hope thought. *Relax, take it easy*. Who was she kidding? This was a professional hitman, and she was trapped inside a shed with him, nowhere to run. If he found her, he could dispatch her. Had he dispatched Victor and Jenna? She doubted it. It was such an amateur job to throw a sound system in, Swen surely could have done it in a much cleaner way. Could you be sure that they would die with the sound system going in? Hope didn't know that much about electricals. Maybe you could.

A torchlight came closer to her and she saw the racks above her being searched. What was he looking for? Again, he searched the rack underneath the first one, and then the one directly on top of Hope. He must surely see her. The light swept just above her. Maybe he couldn't see her in the dark beyond the torchlight. It got like that, didn't it? Especially in total darkness, if you shine a torch, it illuminates what's in front, but the edges become blurred, they become darker, you can't see. God, she hoped he couldn't see.

For a moment, Swen turned away, then he turned back again. His hand reached down, the torch light still held somehow above Hope, but the hand swept the floor underneath the shelf. Hope pulled herself in as tight as she could and could feel the sweat pouring off her face.

Then Swen stood up, walked out of the shed, and closed the door. Hope didn't move. Maybe this was a trick; maybe he was waiting. She remained in position knowing that she would struggle to follow him now, the risk being too great. Before, she was fairly confident that he hadn't seen her. Now, she wondered how he missed her.

It was an hour later before Hope moved. When she opened the door, the first cracks of daylight were beginning to appear, but they were incredibly insignificant compared to the rolling darkness of the storm outside. The difference now was you could begin to see the cloud, the pattern in it, the darks with the whites or the greys as they seemed to be. The rain was still pummelling down hard.

As she got out of the shed, she could see more into the darkness. It was brighter, fewer shadows, and people would be more like figures if she saw someone. She furtively returned to the house entering through the door she had left by. She didn't know where Swen was. Had he made it back? Whatever was happening, he'd been on the move looking for something.

Hope walked back up to her room, stopping a couple of times as she heard some of the servants beginning to pace here and there about the house. When she stepped inside the bedroom she'd been given, she breathed a sigh of relief. Her legs were cold, and she could feel it in the joints of her knees. Once again, she stripped off into a shower, took twenty minutes before coming out, drying herself down, and this time, got into her bed.

What had he been doing out there? she thought. *What was Swen up to? Were they hiding something? Is that what this was all about? Then why would you kill people? Why on earth was he invited here?*

She'd try and sleep for a moment to see if she could get a couple of hours, and then she'd report it all to Macleod. He was probably asleep anyway at this time. She turned over and tried to think of John, but the case kept coming back to her.

Somebody had taken out the head of the house. They had then taken out the new second in command for it would go to the men to start to lead the family again. It confused her. Why was Victor killed? If someone were going after them in terms of the family, Alexei would be next on the list unless they were going for all of the males. Maybe Pavel—was he doing it? Was he trying to put himself in a position?

It was too much. Her brain was tired, and her body was exhausted. Hope pulled the covers around her, grabbed the pillow, and flung her arms around it. It wasn't John, but it was going to have to do.

Chapter 13

Macleod was surprised the next morning when he was invited to breakfast with the family and guests. According to Ivan, his mistress had said it was only fair that Macleod and his team were now looked after in the same way that the guests were. Having no idea where breakfast was going to come from, other than supplied by the Zupci family, Macleod decided that he would accept the invitation and informed the rest of the team. He'd found Hope had been difficult to raise and she spoke to him about Swen and his expedition in the early hours of the morning. Macleod concurred that she'd done the right thing.

'You might have been very lucky,' said Macleod. 'If he had caught you there, effectively catching him red-handed, who knows what would've happened.'

'Have we got any detail on him? Anything we could pull him in for?' asked Hope.

'It's the island that's the problem. Technically we could grab him if we have anything on him but what do we do with him? Mischa isn't going to go for that and then we'll probably get booted off the island and have to go through this much more formally. It would be a delicate matter and the last thing I think we're going to get backing for is to start operating heavy-handed. Whatever it is that our country wants from Zupci, it's enough to override this investigation I'm doing and how I'm doing it. You better get yourself together and we'll head down for breakfast.'

Hope nodded and Macleod left to go to his room while he awaited Clarissa and her to join him. As they made their way down the stairs, Clarissa seemed to be in a good mood.

'What's up with you?' asked Macleod. 'I'd have thought that being kept here from last night would be something to commiserate on. After all, we've got four dead on top of our first body.'

'But you walk down here,' said Clarissa, 'like you don't even know where you are. Look at some of the artwork down this hall. That's stunning. Have you seen the colours in that picture up there? Do you know how old it is?'

'I have no idea,' said Macleod. 'I don't really care. I don't care what the trappings are around us. We have a murder investigation to get on with, but it's hard enough to run it without you looking like you're walking around the best supermarket you've ever seen.'

Clarissa gave him a dirty look. 'Don't start with me like that just because you want to get home. Look, I get it. I really do. But we're here; we're doing a job. Don't blame me for looking at the bright side of it.'

Macleod wanted to apologise, but Clarissa had already stepped away, walking briskly but turning from him as she watched the paintings along the corridor. They arrived on the ground floor of the house and were led into a large room with what Macleod considered to be the biggest dining table he'd ever seen. Many places were set out and some of the guests were already there. Macleod could see fish on the table as well as cereals, milk, fruit, and nearby were several servants ready to attend to their needs.

'Inspector,' said Mischa, standing up from the far end of the table. She was dressed in black, but looked as elegant as ever. Gone from the night before were the tears she was crying. She now looked as if she was simply welcoming a guest to breakfast. 'Thank you for joining us, Inspector. I felt it was the least I could do to offer you some sustenance while you were trapped here.'

'It's very kind,' said Macleod and took up a position at the table far down from Mischa.

'No, indeed not,' she said. 'Come and sit up here by me. You can maybe enlighten me on how things are going.'

'You can enlighten us all,' said Frank, the German sitting far from Mischa. He received a dirty look for his comment and Macleod turned and faced the man.

'I feel that when the time is right, I'll announce to all of you how I'm going. In the meantime, I prefer to keep my counsel to myself.'

'Of course,' said Mischa, sitting down. 'Please, coffee for the inspector. I've been told you like your coffee. Quite the connoisseur in a lot of ways.'

Hope made her way over to sit beside Frank, a decision which he seemed well pleased about. Macleod noticed how she was able to use her own sexuality to place herself into positions of influence without ever actually giving anything away. Macleod wasn't always comfortable with her using her body in this way, but on the other hand, he never had the option. No one ever asked him to come over because he looked good. Clarissa sat down with Lyla Preen, who seemed less than impressed about her companion.

Macleod tasted his coffee put in front of him and realised it was a blend from home that he enjoyed.

'You really do your research, don't you, Madam Zupci?'

'I've told you, it's Mischa. You're my guest here. Please, act like it and less of the officious inspector.'

'With all due respect,' said Macleod quietly, 'you've just lost your husband. You've now lost your son and three other people are dead beyond them. If there was a time for me to act like the officious inspector, it's now.'

'Quite,' said Mischa. 'As you will, but please remember this is my home. This is a place for my guests and not a police station.'

'Indeed, ma'am, and I'd much rather we were at a police station. Hopefully, my forensic officer will be able to get across today.'

'I doubt it,' said Mischa. 'You've seen the weather. We get quite cut off at times here. Quite cut off. I hope it won't stop your investigation, though. We need to find out who is attacking my family.'

'Victor was quite something. Very different, I feel, to your husband.'

'So some would say. I think there were large parts of my husband in Victor. He was a favourite of mine, despite the fact that he wasn't really the most productive of people.'

'I'm sure we would all love our children.'

'You say that so easily, considering you never had any,' Mischa retorted.

'Indeed,' said Macleod. *She knew too much, and was too quick on it,* he thought. She really had investigated her investigator. It struck Macleod that she must have done this incredibly quickly, almost Ross-like in her work.

The door burst opened, and Julie McGeehan marched into the room.

'He grabbed me. He bloody well grabbed me. You need to get that pervert off me.'

Macleod stood up. Hope, too, but Mischa remained seated. 'I beg your pardon? How dare you interrupt our breakfast like this?'

'Get stuffed,' said Julie. 'Your son grabbed me. Damn well groped me. I hope you choke on your breakfast.'

Julie went to turn away, but Hope stepped across and grabbed her. 'Come here,' said Hope. 'What are you saying? Who grabbed you?'

'That pervert, Pavel. He's sat and watched me ever since I arrived. Looking at me, staring at me.'

'What happened?' asked Hope. 'Calm down and just tell me what happened.'

Clarissa had stepped up to flank the woman as well. Macleod saw his team trying to back her up.

'I was getting changed in my room when all of a sudden the door opens and in he comes. He just grabbed me from behind. His hands were, oh, his hands were . . . '

'Hope, can you take Miss McGeehan elsewhere for this?' asked Macleod.

'Of course,' said Hope and ordered Clarissa to join them. As they went to leave the room, Pavel suddenly burst in. His nose was covered in blood, which was pouring down in front of him, staining the simple jumper he had on.

'What the heck?'

'Bastard deserved it,' said Julie. 'Grab me like that, would you? Put your hand on my privates? I gave him a good elbow in the face. Could hear the damn crunch of that nose.'

Pavel had tears streaming from his face, the blood continuing to pour as he ran round towards Mischa. She had now risen to her feet and Macleod had to step lightly to one side to avoid the blood and snot coming from Pavel's nose as Mischa embraced him.

Following him into the room was Kira. She was dressed in black like her mother, elegantly, and had stepped behind Mischa.

'It's true,' said Kira. 'It's true what she says. I had to deal with him. There's a couple of bruises to his face that are from me, not from Miss McGeehan.'

'I think we need to sit everyone down. Take some statements. In fact, best if I took everyone back to Barra,' said Macleod.

'Well, that's not happening, is it, Inspector?' said Mischa. 'You see the weather outside.'

'I can wait,' said Macleod. 'It's not the same as a murder case. We can put your son in a safe room away from Miss McGeehan and then we can deal with the incident off island and take the heat from the situation.'

'You take that wee pervert from the situation is what you need to do,' said Julie.

'I need him at the moment, Inspector,' said Mischa.

'I appreciate your situation, Madam Zupci, but that boy just did something highly inappropriate.'

'I agree, and I shall deal with him.'

'It's not up for you to deal with him.'

'Remember whose land you're on,' said Mischa, suddenly with a sharp tone.

'Remember who you invited here,' said Macleod. 'I'm not a pet. You're not paying me.'

110

I'm just here for justice, thought Macleod. *I'm just here because it's a case and it needs solved.* He began to wonder if he was somehow addicted to this life.

'I think we should take Miss McGeehan outside. I just want to check her over and make sure she's okay,' said Hope. 'We need to diffuse this now.'

'You deny doing this?' Macleod said to Pavel. The boy remained silent. 'I said, do you deny doing this? Miss McGeehan has made an accusation against you.'

The boy whimpered, shaking his head in Mischa's breast.

'He doesn't deny it, Inspector. I think we can resolve this in a better way. Miss McGeehan, I'll double your salary for being here. No, I'll triple it if you say no more of the matter.'

'You can't just buy someone off like that,' said Hope.

Julie McGeehan's hand came out and grabbed Hope's arm. 'I'll speak for myself,' she said quietly. 'Okay. That's okay.'

Macleod's face turned red. 'It's not okay,' he said. 'He's done it to you; he'll do it to someone else at some point.'

'Please, Inspector, the money means more to me than having that little twerp locked up. Won't be long before I'm out of here and never see him again.'

'Well, ultimately, it's up to you,' said Macleod, also aware that if she wanted to press charges, he wasn't quite sure how much backing he'd get from his government. 'But,' Macleod turned to Pavel, 'I get you doing this again and I'll make sure you get hauled in for it, boy. Do you understand?'

Macleod felt bad calling him boy, but he was acting like one, not the man his age said he was. Mischa took Pavel from the room, and Macleod watched Hope and Clarissa escort Julie McGeehan away, probably to her room. He sat down again and saw Frank looking over at him. 'Exciting little place, isn't it?' he said. 'First time you've dealt with the Zupcis, is it?'

'You know it is,' said Macleod.

'She's a law unto herself, that one. All of them. That's the thing about them. Yes, I've made good business out of them, but you need to handle them firmly. You need to take control of what they're doing.'

'Is that what you do, Mr Schmidt? Are you handling them?'

'I see what you did there, Inspector. Very clever. No, I'm not handling them, but I am very wary of them. You should be, too.'

'I'll bear that in mind,' said Macleod.

'As for that one, Pavel, he's weird. Always was. You see, I understand Victor. Oh, far gone. Sex this, sex that. Drugs and debauchery here, there, and everywhere, but I understand him. One of those people in life who just go to excess, but not Pavel. He sees so much that he wants, like Miss McGeehan, but normally, he doesn't touch any of it. He doesn't know how to take command. Doesn't know how to own something. Hence, he just makes a snatch like this, embarrasses his mother and everyone else. He really is the runt of the family.'

'Well, thank you for your insights, Mr Schmidt. I shall continue my inquiries. I also need to know where you were last night.'

'Like I told your Sergeant Urquhart, in my room. Like all of us, in our rooms. Have you not noticed how these things have been done when nobody has an alibi?'

'Yes, I did,' said Macleod. 'That's some planning.'

'It really is,' said Frank. 'It really is, Inspector. I feel you've got your work cut out for you.'

Chapter 14

Macleod picked up the telephone, aware that it was a line coming from the house, and he was about to speak to the assistant chief constable. He wondered how clean the line would be and thought it best to warn his colleague on the other end.

'Jim, it's Seoras. I thought I should update you. It's getting out of hand on this side. I'm not going into too much detail, because it's an open line. It's not even coming through my mobile. I can't get a signal at the moment now.'

'Okay,' said Jim. 'I understand, but what do you mean "It's getting out of hand"?'

'I've got five dead, Jim. The middle son of the Zupci family, his partner, and two entertaining women, shall we say, all found in the Jacuzzi. Somebody lobbed a sound system into it.'

'It couldn't have been accidental?' asked Jim.

'Not when you pick up a sound system from over on the side and launch it into the Jacuzzi. They were all in the Jacuzzi, this is the thing. If one of them had picked it up, they would've been found outside the Jacuzzi. It was definitely deliberate. Definitely an attempt to kill him, or at least one of them who was in the tub.'

'I understand,' said Jim.

'I've also had a sexual assault by the youngest son on the young woman who is doing sports activities here on the island. I'm not happy with this, Jim. I feel like my hands are tied. I'm called in as a what? Some sort of consultant? I'm not operating here as an inspector.'

'I'm afraid that's the rules. Even when you get to the bottom of this, you're just going to be telling Madam Zupci. It'd be up to them what they do with it. The government has said you are in as a consultant.'

'I get that, not happy about it, but it doesn't make it any easier.'

'She asked for you, the government told me to get you, make sure you're there. Get in, get the job done, get out,' said Jim. 'That's all I can offer you. If you come away now, the government's going to be pissed. We're going to get a load of hassle. Do you need any extra manpower?'

'They'll not get here for a day or two anyway. A storm is blowing through.'

'Do you feel at risk at all?'

Macleod wanted to say, 'Of course I do. I've got a hit man on the Island. I'm here with a load of gangsters,' but he couldn't. Not over an open line like this. Who knew who was listening. 'Let's just say the waters are a little tepid,' said Macleod, hoping that Jim would get the meaning from his voice.

'Get it done, get out. How is Jane?'

'I'm just going to ring her. I'll be in touch, Jim. I'll try and wrap this up as quick as we can, but to be honest, we have a heck of a lot of suspects here.'

'Understood, Seoras. Call me if you need anything else.'

Macleod put the phone down, picked it up immediately, and began to ring Jane. On the other end of the line, a male voice answered.

'This is Jane's phone. Angus speaking.'

'Angus, how are you? It's Seoras here.'

'Ah, Inspector.'

'It's Seoras. Ross works for me; you don't. How is she?'

'She's as well as can be expected, Seoras, but yes, it's not easy. We're getting somewhere. I think she's appreciating the company.'

'Well, I do. It's good knowing somebody's there just in case she has a problem, or God forbid, somebody else should have a problem with her.'

'I'll go and get her to speak to you. Assume you probably don't have much time.'

'That I don't,' said Macleod. 'Thank you.'

He heard the phone being placed down, and Angus could be heard walking along Macleod's wooden hall floor. Macleod sat waiting for Jane to come onto the line, but then he thought that the silence had changed. Normally, on the phone, if you were waiting for someone, you heard something in the background. The line had suddenly nothing on it.

'Hello?' said Macleod. 'Anybody there? Hello? Hello?' He waited another minute. No one had come back. 'Hello? This is Seoras. Jane, you there? Jane, you there?'

Nothing. He put the phone down, picked it back up again, listening for the dial tone, but there was nothing at all. He placed the phone back in its cradle and walked off, looking for Ivan. Instead, he found one of the other servants, and irately announced that the phone wasn't working, and they needed another one. The man looked and shook his head, but

115

Macleod railed at him again, causing the man to run off, and Ivan returned shortly.

'What's the problem, Inspector?'

'Your phone's not working. Can you get me another one?' Ivan indicated that Macleod should follow him, turned around another corridor, and picked up another phone. Handing it to him. Macleod pressed the green button. There was no sound on the phone.

'How do you work these things?' said Macleod. 'There's not a phone line coming through.'

Ivan took it, pressed it to his ear, then pressed several buttons again, and put it back to his ear. 'The phone is working. It appears the phone lines are not.'

As he turned to put the phone back onto its cradle, Macleod saw Ivan suddenly go into darkness. Despite being daytime, the dark clouds, and the storm outside caused the house to be dark, so the lights had been switched on. This particular corridor they were in was in the depths of the house, so when the power went from the lights, Ivan suddenly became a mere blur to Macleod.

'Sorry, Inspector. I must go and see if everyone's all right. I have things to do at a time like this.'

'Do you have a generator, a separate source?'

'Nothing that could run a house like this. We have a small generator, but that's to keep fridges going and things like that. Some of the freezers and fridges are well stocked. We must look to that first, but we still get candles out and light the house up. Get some fires going. We'll be okay in that sense, Inspector, but you must let me go to work.'

'Of course,' said Macleod, and stepped aside to let the man go. Macleod traipsed back slowly in the dark towards his room and met Hope in the corridor.

'Where are you going?' she asked.

'Just back to my room. The lights have gone. Power's gone; the phone line's down. I was going to sit down and think.'

'I've just come from speaking to Frank, and many of the other guests, and it's like the first killing, Seoras. Everybody's on their own. Everybody's with their partner or on their own. Nobody can vouch for anyone else at the time the killing takes place, even up to half an hour before. We were packing up; everybody else was going out up to their rooms before they were going to come down for dinner. Nobody had made it out of their rooms. It's perfect timing.'

'This is perfect timing too, isn't it? We can't get Jona over. We can't even communicate to get her over. Who knows when she's coming over when the storm subsides. I'm probably going to struggle to know when the storm's going to subside now. Well, they did say a couple of days.'

Hope nodded. 'Maybe it's Swen,' she said. 'Maybe he's taking them out one by one.'

'But who for?' said Macleod. 'And why am I here? I still don't get that. I don't like how quickly I've been assigned here. How quickly after her husband's death, I'm getting the call and I'm coming down. That doesn't work for me.'

'Also why is Swen here?' said Hope. 'Why would you invite a person who's a contract killer? If we know it, if we know he is a hitman, they must know it. They're deeper into that world than we'll ever get.'

'How's Julie McGeehan?' asked Macleod.

'She seems all right. A bit of a fright. I can understand it. That Pavel's looked at me a few times and not in a nice way. I think Julie's an ordinary woman. I mean, I don't think she'd mind the odd glance from a person, but she said that Pavel, every time he came to any of the events she was running, he'd just stand and stare at her. Frank said he's a freak.'

'Frank's very communicative,' said Macleod. 'It seems he wants to give his opinion on everybody to me and to you.' There was a tap from Macleod's shoulder and he nearly jumped, realising Clarissa had snuck up on him.

'Well, he's right on that situation,' said Clarissa. 'Pavel is a pervert. Standing and staring at a woman like that and sneaking into her room and grabbing her. There's no other word for it. He's not weird. He's beyond that.'

'Hope thinks Swen might be behind it. What do you think?' Macleod asked Clarissa.

'What I think is we're incredibly exposed here and we shouldn't be getting too far away from each other.'

'You think we're under threat,' said Macleod.

'Don't you, Seoras?'

'No,' said Macleod. 'I don't. I don't think anything's going to happen to us. We're here for a purpose.'

'To solve a crime,' said Clarissa. 'Well, we know that police officers do go down in line of duty though.'

'Not here they don't. Think about it. What good does it do anybody if we die? We've been sent in to help. If somebody takes us out, that's a major problem. It's going to bring in lots and lots of heat. At the moment, this is on Zupci's rules, not on the UK's terms. I think that's where people want to keep playing it. They don't want me to come in as part of the UK government leaping all over them. In fact, if it gets that serious, they won't send me in, will they? Then suddenly we'll get somebody like Kirsten coming in to deal with it. The rules will be very different. I'm the softly, softly approach.'

Clarissa was laughing. 'When have you ever been the softly, softly approach? And anyway, you brought your work file with you, didn't you?'

'I did,' he said quietly. 'Maybe it's time to let you loose a bit. Maybe it's time we all got a little bit looser on this.'

'Inspector.' A voice rang down the corridor. Macleod turned to see Mischa at the far end. 'Would you join me? I need to talk to you.'

'Just a moment,' said Macleod. 'I'm just finishing up with my sergeants. The three of us will be with you directly.'

'No, Inspector, just yourself, if you please.'

Macleod turned back and raised his eyebrows at his two sergeants. 'Stick together,' he said. 'Let's try and stay safe but to be honest, I think we're part of a show. I'll go and see what I can find out.'

Macleod turned from his sergeants and walked down the corridor to meet Mischa at the far end. She was wearing a thin black skirt that came more than halfway up towards her knees. It was tight fitting, but elegant and along with the lace black top she was wearing, she cut quite a dashing figure. However, she appeared to be charming towards Macleod rather than have any other intention.

'This way, Inspector,' she said, opening a door into a small sitting room. She placed herself on a long sofa but tapped beside herself to where Macleod should sit down. As he did so, a servant appeared at one of the doors. 'A glass of sherry for the inspector,' said Mischa.

'I'd rather have a coffee,' said Macleod, and thought he'd just seen the first thing she'd got wrong about him.

'My apologies. I thought you were one of those quiet drinkers, only for the intimate moments or on your own.'

'I'm not on my own,' said Macleod, 'and it's certainly not an intimate moment.'

Mischa's hand moved across onto his thigh. 'I think all our moments are intimate but, of course, coffee,' she said, lifting her hand back off. Macleod watched her stand and walk over to a window while they waited for the coffee to arrive. Once it came, it was poured for him and he took a sip, realising once again it was the brand he desired. The servant left the room and Mischa turned around to him, putting her hands on a table and leaning towards him in an elegant fashion.

'Do you think that my family is being targeted?'

'Considering your husband and your second son are dead, I find it highly likely,' said Macleod. 'It's not really a large deduction. The two women who were hired by Victor in some ways are superfluous and I got the feeling that Jenna was not really that welcome around here.'

'Jenna was Victor's choice. She wouldn't have been the choice of my husband. Well, not as a partner. He was quite a loving man to his family but he did have his weaknesses. I can't deny that, and Victor unfortunately inherited most of them.'

'You think it's somebody inside your family?'

'Never,' said Mischa, suddenly and sharply. She marched over to Macleod, stood over him looking down. 'Don't ever say that.'

'Well, apologies,' said Macleod, 'but given the history of the Royal Family in my nation, especially if you look back into earlier days, they weren't the best behaved. I'm wondering if your family is.'

'That's really quite rude for someone that's entertaining you.'

'Pavel?' said Macleod.

'Pavel is very troubled,' said Mischa, suddenly turning away. 'He struggled having a strong father, but I do wonder if maybe Frank is coming for us, or someone else. The men, you see, that's who holds the power in our family. That's how it works. It's passed down. It's not like your changing country. I fear they want to wipe out all of the men, make an example.'

'Well, why don't you have more security here?'

'I have security enough, trust me, but I need you to get to the bottom of who's doing this. If you call it, everyone will not see it as a stitch-up by us. There are people back home who think we would take advantage of this situation. I just want to protect my family. You do believe me on that, Inspector?'

Macleod looked up at the woman. He scanned her eyes and her face. Her lips were tight, pursed together as if she needed to make him understand.

'Indeed,' said Macleod. 'It's one thing I'm definitely sure of.'

Chapter 15

Despite the absence of power, Macleod continued his investigations, re-interviewing everyone as best he could. The weather outside was atrocious; continued high winds and heavy rain made it impossible for the island to be serviced by any boats. What generators were available were currently being used to maintain the kitchens, specifically the freezer area, and all lighting within the house was being produced by candlelight. Macleod thought it gave the place an air of grandeur, but also many dark corners, and he noted that many times when he was in the corridor, he struggled to catch people's faces clearly.

The little objects, paintings that had previously adorned the halls, each bathed in a separate light provided by its own specific fixture, were now just pieces in the shadows, much to Clarissa's disgust. She had mentioned several times to Macleod how easy it would be to walk off with any of them until he pointed out that while the thief could get outside the house, getting off the island would be a completely different story.

Despite the difficulties of the weather, the entertainment for the house guests continued with Julie McGeehan leading a fitness session in a candlelit hall and a large billiards room was occupied by those of a more sedate nature. Copious drink was supplied to keep away the melancholy blues that had surrounded most of the guests. Despite chatting with them and despite asking at times some quite invasive questions, Macleod found he was getting nowhere. One of the biggest problems was tying down where everyone was during both murders, having both happened late on. Everyone was apparently in their beds or rooms, something Macleod didn't believe, but he did feel he was up against it as many of these people would have lied to police before.

With the power out, Mischa's attitude to Macleod had also seemed to soften. She requested that he attend dinner that night with the rest of the guests and she included Clarissa and Hope in that invite as well. When Macleod approached Clarissa's room, he knew she would be excited, as if things were finally being done properly. He rapped the door.

'You can come in, I'm decent.'

She had such a way with words. Despite the fine company she could keep, Clarissa could be incredibly down to earth.

'I can get used to this,' she said. 'Staff took them away, cleaned them up today despite all the power being out. I mean, look at it. Shawl looks fantastic. It's almost better than I could get it to come up.'

Macleod ignored her comment, instead wondering at the pile of makeup that lay out on the table. Jane had her own collection, but Macleod deliberately kept away from it. Jane had her time when she got made up, as she put it, and that time was generally spent by Macleod out on the garden or reading something downstairs. He never had asked or pried into what she did and why she did it; he just gave her that compliment when she came down the stairs.

'If you're ready, we'll pick up Hope and get down. I don't want to miss any of the chat. It might be where we pick up what's going on here. Hopefully with a bit of alcohol, they might talk a bit looser.'

'It's good you see the benefits of alcohol at last,' said Clarissa and received a raised eyebrow from Macleod. 'You do know this is the sort of investigation I used to get involved in, high-priced art. With the police, but before that, working with insurance companies.'

'I didn't know you'd worked that often with insurance companies. They'd said you had a couple of outings; that was on the notes.'

'Nearly five years on and off, half seconded. Some of the bigger arts thefts and that. To be honest, we needed to work alongside them. Some of the resources and money they had, fantastic, but then again, they'd been paying out millions when they got it wrong. But when you went out for your dinner that night with those guys, it wasn't a kebab round the back of somewhere. No, they knew how to eat . . . classy.'

'Well, I'm sorry we don't cater for that, but come on, let's go.'

Macleod left the room without waiting for Clarissa. Stepping across the corridor, he banged on Hope's door. His sergeant emerged looking distinctly underdressed compared to Clarissa; that wasn't unusual. Whilst Clarissa was dressed up in a tartan shawl and had made the effort to spruce herself up for dinner, Hope was wearing her blue jeans, black T-shirt, leather jacket, with her red hair tied up behind her. She looked like she was attending any case.

'You ready?' asked Macleod.

'Of course. I was just running through a few things. Can't get any mobile contact. Are the phones still down?'

'Pretty much,' said Macleod. 'They haven't even got satellite phone here. That's what's surprising me.'

'Satellite phone that you know about.' Macleod turned and looked at Clarissa.

'Well, think about it, I mean they must have. What about boats? Could you get Channel sixteen and get the Coastguard, get the message through that way? Even get to talk to Ross on a line like that.'

'Never thought about boats. They must have a boat here surely. I mean, what do they do when they want off the island?'

'Fly,' said Hope. 'They have a helicopter set up over at Barra airport. That's how they get on and off. They bring the boats over for supplies and that, or to take the staff here and there. So, you're out of luck. There're no boats here at the moment. I did ask.'

'Of course, you did,' said Macleod, and he turned back to Clarissa. 'That's why she's my number one.'

'Yes. You just wanted the younger model,' laughed Clarissa, causing Macleod to frown. He gave a glance at Hope. He could see her broad smile. That was the thing with Clarissa; she knew where everybody was at, so when she made jokes, they were taken in good humour. Unless, of course, she intended to get at you. Then they came with barbs attached.

Macleod made his way down to the large dining room where a servant opened the doors and announced him in such a formal fashion that Macleod felt he'd won an award. Once again, he was invited to sit near Mischa, who tonight was resplendent in a silvery gown. Macleod noted that all the guests were looking rather spruced up. Even Swen was there in a tuxedo while in his shirt and tie, Macleod felt very underdressed. Hope and Clarissa sat amongst the other guests, while Mischa leaned in at first, asking Macleod how he was getting on with the investigations. She may have thought he was evading her but in truth, he didn't have much to tell, and soon she leaned away and started engaging the rest of her guests.

'We'll just wait for Pavel,' said Mischa. Macleod had noticed that the young man hadn't arrived. Alexei and Karina were there, and they looked distinctly nervous. The rest of the guests gave pleasant enough nods. Macleod noticed that Swen didn't speak but instead, Frank was the life and soul of the table. He caused Macleod to raise his eyebrows when he started talking about a deal he'd made with the former Duke.

'Of course, we were in Latvia at the time. Had a little backwater spa. Well, I wouldn't say if he was here but at the time he liked his entertainment, and these particular entertainers out in Latvia were very entertaining indeed.'

'I'm not sure you should bring that sort of thing up in front of my mother,' said Alexei.

'She knew fine well what your father was.'

'I happen to agree with my son,' said Mischa. 'Not really the place to talk like that.' She flicked her eyes over towards Kira, who was sitting quietly at the top of the table.

'As if your kids don't know. Half of them take after him anyway.'

There was a sudden silence in the table. Macleod caught Mischa's eye and could see the rage rising up inside her. Alexei started to raise his hand but instead, Kira looked down the table, staring intently at Frank. Macleod noticed that Swen had started to look a little uneasy.

'Well, he was,' said Frank. 'He liked the ladies. You must have known, Mischa. Everyone knew. His mother knew. Back in the day before you, Yulia used to complain to me about him. She wanted to see him married to somebody strong, somebody good. He got that in you, but you got a randy sort in return. Can't have been easy,' said Frank suddenly. 'Some of the things he got up to.'

'You will not speak ill of my father,' said Kira suddenly.

'Ill of him? It's just the way he was,' said Frank. 'Every business trip with him, he wanted a girl on his arms. I'm sorry, my dear, but that's the way he was. Half of your brothers are like that as well. Victor, especially. I mean, look at the way he went out. Sure, there's many a man would've enjoyed to go that way.'

'Enough,' said Mischa. 'Enough.'

'Why enough?' said Sarah Kurtz. 'I gave the Duke pleasure. Lyla did, too. That's the way you did it when you were a woman; that's the favours he wanted to get on anywhere.'

'And we're not complaining,' said Sarah. 'He did all right for me. He did good.'

'You don't need to rub it in my mother's face,' said Alexei.

'We don't need to,' said Sarah. 'Your brother does it, Pavel and that young trainer. What is he like with her? At least your father had a bit of discretion about him. Victor took it off to his own room. Pavel, he's got no standards, no idea what to do.'

'Enough,' said Mischa. 'You're guests here.'

'Indeed, we are,' said Frank. 'Indeed, we are, and why are we guests here? What's this all about? You keep entertaining us, despite the fact that your husband has died, your son is dead.'

Mischa slammed a fist down on the table and stood up. Macleod saw her draw her shoulders back and stare down towards Frank. 'Whoever did that will be brought to justice.'

'Is that the point?' asked Sarah. 'To hold us here, hold us here until you find out who? And then what? That was the Duke's way as well, wasn't it?'

Macleod thought about interrupting but there seemed to be a lot of forthright comments being made, comments you wouldn't make in front of a police officer.

'Where is the little perv tonight, anyway?' said Frank. 'He probably took the biggest part of your husband.'

'You're lucky his mother isn't here. You're lucky Yulia isn't in this room.'

'Why?' said Frank.

'Because she's old school,' said Mischa. 'She wouldn't say anything to you, but you'd be made an example of. It's people like her our fortune was built on.'

'It certainly wasn't your husband,' said Frank. 'Number of situations we had to cover up for him, unbelievable. I still have no idea how you took over that country. Anyway,' he said, 'I'm starving. Can we eat?'

'We wait for Pavel,' said Mischa. 'He's part of the family and he'll be here to eat. Ivan, advise my son we are ready for him.'

Macleod saw Ivan snap to attention and suddenly march out of the room. There was a quiet in the air and he could see people looking back and forward at each other. He caught Hope's eye. She had raised her eyebrows up, almost to ask him, 'What on earth was that?' Looking at Clarissa, he saw a wry smile on her lips. It was almost as if she'd enjoyed that.

It was three minutes later when Ivan walked back into the room and Macleod could read the worry on his face straight away, but the man walked up the side of the table quietly, bent down, leaned into Mischa, and whispered something. Macleod leaned over. 'What is it?'

'Ivan said Pavel's door is locked. He can't get any response from him.' Macleod was out of his seat before she'd finished speaking. 'McGrath, Urquhart, with me. Ivan, have you got a key for that door?'

The guests looked bewildered, and Ivan shook his head.

'It's his bedroom. He has the key. He doesn't allow any of the staff to have one.'

'Send for an axe just in case we need it.'

'What the heck's going on?' said Frank. 'What is he doing now? What's the little Pavel pervert up to?'

Macleod ignored him, marched out of the large double doors of the dining room, out into the corridor, and suddenly stopped. He had no idea where Pavel's room was.

'Ivan, lead the way.'

'With me, Seoras,' said Clarissa, marching past him. 'Been all over this house. Inside out. That's what happens when you're number two,' she said quietly as they went up to the stairs. 'You get sent to all the places. All the spade work. All the . . . '

'Shut up,' said Macleod. 'I don't think he's locked himself in his room.'

Clarissa looked over. 'Oh,' she said and began to speed up as best she could.

When they arrived on the landing with Pavel's room, Macleod could see a servant at the far end already knocking the door.

'Stand aside please, sir,' said Macleod on arrival, raised his fist and thundered it against the door. 'It's Detective Inspector Macleod. Are you in there, Pavel? I need to know if you're in there. If you don't tell us we're going to break in. We're concerned about your safety, sir, concerned that something may have happened to you. So, if you're fine, please answer or

129

please open the door.'

There was silence from the other side and Macleod heard more people coming up the stairs behind him.

'Clarissa, cover those stairs. Don't let anybody come closer unless it's someone with an axe.'

Clarissa nodded and Macleod pointed to the door looking at Hope. 'I'm not going to break it in,' he said. 'Do you want to give it go?' Hope looked at the door, wooden but modern and new.

'Not unless you want me to sully my shoulder with a large bruise,' said Hope. 'Where's the axe?'

She turned and saw Clarissa stepping aside as Ivan appeared with an axe. Macleod stood back as Hope took it, launching it into the door, cutting away where the lock was. As splintered wood lay on the floor, the door slid open into a darkened room inside. Macleod watched Hope walk over to a shadowy figure on the bed. She checked his pulse and his breathing and walked back to Macleod at the edge of the room and said quietly in his ear, 'Pavel's dead, Seoras, and it looks like somebody stuck him with a knife.'

Chapter 16

'Where is he? Where is my Pavel?'

Macleod could hear Mischa outside. 'You stay in here, McGrath. Don't let anyone in until we calm this situation down.' Macleod stepped quickly outside the room, saw Mischa running over in her silvery dress. Clarissa was holding back the rest of the crowd and he saw Alexei trying to push through past her.

'Where is Pavel?' said Mischa. 'Where is my Pavel?'

Macleod stepped forward, holding his hands up. 'Don't. Don't go in there.'

'No,' the woman shrieked. 'No.'

She tore towards the door, Macleod stepping across, grabbing her, putting his arms around her waist, holding her back. The woman was strong, though, and Macleod could feel himself being dragged back towards the room.

'The Inspector's correct, don't go in there.'

Hope had joined Macleod. As Macleod looked up, he saw Alexei pushing Clarissa over to one side. She fell back, smacking her head off the wall as the mass of people on the stairs suddenly rushed forward.

'That doorway. Get in that doorway,' Macleod said to

McGrath.

'What's happened to the little pervert?' shouted Frank.

'Everyone, stay back,' said Macleod. 'Back, now.'

He knew he was losing though and Mischa broke from him, running towards the door. Alexei was joining her, and he stepped in front of his mother.

'Get out of the way or I'll kick you out of the way.'

Macleod turned and watched as Alexei slapped Hope across the face. 'Out of the way, woman.'

It was almost a blur as she did it, but Hope got hold of the man's wrist, spun him around, put an arm up his back and put him down on his knees on the floor at a speed which caused Mischa to jump back from the Sergeant. Then she realised that Hope was occupied at this time and there was a gap in the door. Macleod made a grab for her arm, but he couldn't stop Mischa running into the room. He skipped past Hope, followed her, shouting behind him, 'Urquhart, lend a hand.'

Mischa screamed, the cry of a mother that went right down to Macleod's core. She'd always seemed more in control with the other deaths, but this one seemed to grab her. He placed his arms on her shoulders.

'Time to go. Time to go.'

He watched as she bowed her head. He could hear sobbing, and then the drops falling on the floor.

'No,' she said, reaching towards Pavel, but Macleod held her back.

'You can't,' he said. 'You can't; you'll contaminate the scene. If we have any chance of catching whoever did this . . . '

Macleod heard Alexei yell. 'One of them. It'll be one of them. Frank.' Macleod became more forceful with Mischa, turning her, edging her back towards the door.

'Stop assaulting my officer and look after your mother,' Macleod barked at Alexei, nodding at Hope to let him go. The man slowly got to his feet, staring at Hope before letting his mother put her head on his shoulder.

'Is he dead?' asked Frank from the rear.

Macleod held up his hands as an uproar began again.

'Quiet! Quiet and listen! Someone has murdered Pavel in the room behind me. No one will go into that room. Ivan, get some servants and escort the rest of these people back downstairs. I want you to stay in the dining room where I can come down and speak to you about your movements before tonight.'

'Like hell,' said Frank. 'Like hell I'm staying in here.'

'You're right,' said Sarah Kurtz. 'You're right. You're insane, Inspector. You think we're going to hang around here just to get killed?'

'It's not you who are getting killed,' said Alexei. 'It's my family. It's us. It's probably one of you who're doing it.'

'And it's that attitude,' said Frank, 'that means I'm getting out of here before you come for us.'

'There's nowhere to go,' said Macleod calmly. 'The weather's closed in. There's no boat. There's no helicopter. We are on this island. We can't contact anyone.'

'Isn't that bloody convenient?' said Frank.

Macleod saw Clarissa stumbling over towards him, her hand up behind her head. As she drew closer, she whispered in his ear, 'What do you want me to do?' He saw her taking her hand off the back of her head and he could see the blood on it.

'Ivan, get one of your staff to go and get a cloth. Cold compress. My officer needs attention.'

Ivan remained calm amidst all of this, turning, issuing

instructions and Macleod saw the servants running here and there. None of them were like Ivan. Ivan gave the impression this is what happened every day but the other servants had faces of panic.

Hope leaned across to Macleod. 'What do we do now?'

'We man the battlements until they withdraw. No one gets in that room. Nobody gets to sully that evidence.'

Hope gave a nod, repositioning herself back in the doorway. Macleod was struggling. Jona couldn't get out here. Jona didn't even know this had happened. He'd be without forensics. He already had bodies covered up, preserved as best he could downstairs in Victor's rooms, but now he had another one. How long would the storm be? Another day? Two? He couldn't even look up the weather on his phone.

Maybe they could pick up a radio. Maybe there was a way to broadcast. These people had cut themselves off in the storm. Everyone knew what the islands were like. The weather out here could turn like this; communications could go down. There must have been some way that they would have to communicate. They had an empire, after all, a criminal empire to run.

'And is this the best you're going to do, Inspector?' said Frank. 'Send us back down? Send us back down to sit and wait amongst people who think we killed their family? Well, it's not happening.'

'As I've already said, where are you going to go?'

'There's a small beach building. We can go down there.'

'Good idea,' said Sarah. 'We can go down there, lock ourselves in. Lock ourselves in until somebody comes, get a boat or a helicopter and get the hell out of here. Before something happens to us. You heard it today. The Duke used to play around with us. Frank knows enough about this family to bury half of them.'

Mischa looked up off her son's shoulder. 'And did you? Have you? Is this yours? We had good business, good business.'

'I paid for that business and the women and the drugs and the booze I gave your husband. You know he was never good at business.'

Kira suddenly stepped forward from amongst the mass of bodies.

'May I see him, Inspector?' she said.

'In a moment,' said Macleod. 'I'll accompany you in a moment, but I need to calm this situation first.'

The young girl was quiet and stepped to one side, reaching her hand out and taking her mother's in hers. Karina, Alexei's partner, marched up to Macleod.

'You need to solve this quick. You need to show us which one of these bastards killed our family.'

'Enough,' said Macleod. 'Enough posturing from everyone. Go downstairs and await me.'

'You can come and find me.'

'Nobody's going anywhere, Frank,' said Macleod. 'Nobody.'

'No, if Frank feels safer then by all means. Ivan,' said Mischa, looking around. Once again, the man magically appeared from amongst everyone. 'Give Frank the key. If Miss Kurtz wants to go with him, then by all means. You can, of course, go and see them, Inspector.'

Mischa was rallying in a truly remarkable fashion. 'Anyone else can return downstairs and begin dinner. We could all do with some food at the moment. Ivan, make sure that everyone is looked after. Ivan, food and things like that out to the small house as well. Make sure they have fuel, logs and whatever else they need.'

Ivan nodded and it occurred to Macleod that he would be the busiest man around here, possibly busier than himself in the next couple of hours.

It took fifteen minutes before the landing was clear of everyone except Kira. Alexei had taken his mother downstairs, but Kira had waited and Macleod showed her into the room, cautioning her to keep at a distance from the body of her brother. He watched as she stared at him, a small tear forming in her eye, which ran down her cheek before dribbling off the end of her chin. She reached up and wiped it with a neat, white handkerchief.

'Do you know who did this?' she asked Macleod softly.

'I have my suspicions,' said Macleod, but in his head, he thought those suspicions included just about everybody who had been out on that landing.

'What about the McGeehan girl?' said Kira. 'Pavel was annoying her.'

'She wasn't here, of course,' said Macleod.

'And she wasn't at the table either. An employee.'

'That's a possibility,' said Macleod, 'but one of many.'

After giving Kira a few moments to stay and look at her brother, he escorted her back downstairs to the dining room. The table was missing two occupants, Frank and Sarah Kurtz having departed for the beach house. To the rest of them, Macleod gave a short address, advising them to stay together, to always be with someone and not to be on their own.

'Don't, Inspector,' said Mischa. 'These are my guests, and you can't run an investigation like that. These are my guests and we shall not run this house like a police station.'

'No,' said Macleod, 'but if you want to remain safe, you'll do it.'

'They're still my guests. This is still my family, and they will come and go as they please.'

Macleod shook his head and then checked in with Clarissa, making sure that the wound at the back of her head was healing.

'Quite the bump. When they took you downstairs . . . ?'

'Yes, I asked about Julie McGeehan. Julie's been down with staff all day. She hasn't been out of sight. She did her workout with a guest and one of the staff helped her put her equipment away and then she came down and started to eat with the staff. Pavel had been seen looking at Julie from a distance before she started her workout. One of the staff told me that. She hasn't been out of sight of anyone since then.'

'We need to get onto everyone else, find out where they were, but I'm suspecting with the power cut, people would have been disappearing. I mean, we were back up in our rooms. People were getting changed for dinner.'

'Once again, though,' said Clarissa, 'that's three murder scenes. Three occasions and we can't eliminate anyone except Julie McGeehan and that's because she's with the staff.'

'And she's got no reason to do this,' said Macleod. 'She's just been hired. From what I gathered, she didn't advertise specifically for this job. They went and picked her.'

'I wonder if Pavel was involved in that. He did seem obsessed with her.'

'Well, we'll not get to ask him, Clarissa. We need to start moving quickly, though. We need to get to the bottom of this. I fear that with the power out, things are going to accelerate. We have two brothers down and their father. Somebody seems to be systematically wiping out the men in this family.'

'Is your thinking it's a business rival or a gang rival of some sort, somebody who wants to demolish their line? Somebody who wants to stop them. It is all about the male heir, isn't it?' said Clarissa. 'The women here, they're very much backseat.'

'Backseat, but in control, steering, dominating. I mean, who would you choose to run the family, looking at them?' asked Macleod.

'Probably Mischa. Alexei is better than the other two, but . . .'

'But he's got a strong woman behind him pushing him. Mischa, maybe,' said Macleod, 'but she wasn't that strong, was she? Especially with everyone talking about the Duke's indiscretions.'

Macleod looked back at the dining room before him, feeling hungry, for he hadn't been able to eat yet. He looked across at Alexei and could see the worry on the man's face. His arm was stretched out under the table, and he saw that Karina's was also stretched out to him. There was fear in both their eyes. Macleod understood why.

Chapter 17

M acleod was ready to swing at someone. He was stuck on this island with no forensic backup in a situation where he wasn't completely up to date on what jurisdiction he had, although he believed it was practically nothing. He now was incommunicado with the very people he wanted to complain at. He'd been dumped in this situation, felt that the Zupcis had played whatever card they held over his government to make him come there to deduce what was happening.

The evening had not gone particularly well. Macleod had interviewed everyone to find out where they were when Pavel must have died. They knew Pavel had been there looking at Julie McGeehan at the start of her session for the guests. Then he'd gone to his room. Within that point of time, the only person that Macleod could rule out from having killed Pavel was Julie McGeehan, the very person people were trying to put the blame on. It ran through his head that the whole thing might have been staged around Julie, but yet Pavel was quite clearly obsessed with her.

Julie McGeehan herself was in a mess. She was worried what the family would do, but Macleod had told her and them that she hadn't done it. Therefore, she was innocent and Mischa had seemed to accept this, albeit reluctantly. Macleod had advised Julie to stay with the staff in the house, to be around people at all times. Although he didn't feel she was under threat, he was worried that she might get involved in other things due to being in a panicked state.

Clarissa was feeling somewhat better, the bang on the head only leaving her pride wounded. She'd worked hard with Hope to take down all the details of where everyone had been and the current mood. At best it was a very edgy household. Frank and Sarah had moved out and Macleod was determined to see them the following day. Before they had left, he had insisted on speaking with them, finding out where they were. Yes, they'd attended Julie McGeehan's session, but then they'd gone back to their rooms individually and therefore were still up as suspects.

Macleod was having trouble with Frank. Why was he here? He clearly had issues with the family before and yet he'd come on his own. No bodyguards, nothing, with a family he seemingly had to be careful around.

By the time everyone had gone to bed that night, the place had gone quieter. You could still feel the tension, the fear, but the outbursts had stopped. Sitting in his room with a lone candle burning beside his bed, Macleod tried to sit and think through what was happening, tried to see the people behind the situation, not just the timeframe, not simply where everyone had been. Somebody was wearing a mask here. Somebody was a killer.

There came a rap at Macleod's door, and he shoved his legs out of bed, walked slowly over and asked quietly through the door who it was.

'It's Hope, Seoras.' He opened the door and watched as his redheaded sergeant entered the room, dressed in track bottoms and a t-shirt.

'I thought you were going to bed. What time is it? Two?'

'Swen's on the move. I've just seen him outside. I'm going to tail him, see where he's going. '

'Not on your own, you're not,' said Macleod, dressed in his pyjamas.

'No, we can't both go,' said Hope. 'Something happens to the pair of us, what? Clarissa's left on her own? We're both in charge. It's not wise.'

'No,' said Macleod. 'It's not. Take Clarissa with you.'

'I can handle it myself.'

'You said it before, Swen's a hitman. More awkward with two people. Besides, you'll find Clarissa's not too shabby when it comes to things like this.'

'How do you mean?'

'Think about it, Hope. Look at Clarissa, she can't tail people easily. She can't sneak around. She works from a distance and with a hitman, a distance is the best place to be.'

Hope protested, but Macleod insisted. Two minutes later, Clarissa was standing in Macleod's room as well.

'Look out the window,' said Hope. Macleod peered down into the darkness. There were no lights outside due to the power being out, but there was a figure in the dark, not far from the back door.

'Get going then,' said Macleod. After Hope left the room, Macleod whispered over to Clarissa, 'Take care of her.'

Hope descended the stairs, looking around to see Clarissa following her. Once she got to the rear door of the house, she opened it slowly, looking outside. Swen had moved on. Hope looked up at Macleod's window, where she saw a candle and Macleod's hand pointing over to the east.

'Come on,' said Hope to Clarissa. 'It's out that way.'

'It's not easy to see. The ground's pretty rough, too.'

'Shh,' said Hope. 'We're on the trail. Can you keep it quiet?'

Clarissa felt the wind nearly lift her off her feet, as it howled around the house. 'Quiet?' she said. 'I could have a Mardi Gras band following him here and he wouldn't hear them.'

Hope crouched down alone in the darkness, then stopped and turned to see Clarissa stomping away across the grass. *Unbelievable*, thought Hope. *How did Macleod think she was going to sneak around with her?*

It took a few minutes before Hope saw an outline of Swen skulking behind one of the buildings before making a direct line out towards the beach house where Frank and Sarah were. Hope tried to keep up as Swen moved quickly through the grass, up and down over the uneven terrain. Several times she looked back to see Clarissa struggling along, her shawl blowing around in the wind.

As Swen got closer to the house, Hope decided she couldn't wait, worried that the man was going to carry out a hit. She watched as he went to the front door of the beach house, saw him work at whatever locks were there and quietly step inside. Hope followed as closely as she could, peering in at several windows to see where Swen was. He was walking through the house quite deliberately, slowly, and Hope raced to the front door, opening it, sneaking in as quietly she could.

She got down on her knees, crawling along behind a sofa, before she saw Swen move over to one of the doors. He opened it, looked around, then closed it again. Whoever he was after clearly wasn't in that room. Swen was tall, but he was light on his feet as he walked across to the bedroom on the other side of the beach house. Hope saw him open the door, then reach inside his jacket. He took something out in his hand and entered.

Hope stood up quickly. She opened the bedroom door, peering, trying to find Swen. She couldn't. She looked over and saw Frank lying in his bed. She froze for a moment and then she saw the shape, the figure on the far side of the bed. Hope made a sudden dash around the wooden bed frame to leap and grab Swen. However, he was ready for her and caught her as she approached, turning her around and putting his arm around her neck and driving her down to the ground. Together, the two of them were hunched over as Swen held her tight and she felt his arm slowly choking her, quietly, with a hand over her mouth.

It seemed like she was struggling for a good half minute, and she could feel the air leaving her. Things started to get slower, and she thought soon she would pass out.

There was an almighty crash. Swen's arm fell off her and the big man fell to one side winding up on the floor. Hope looked up and saw Clarissa holding the remains of a pot in her hand.

'What the hell!' yelled Frank, suddenly jumping out of bed.

'I don't wish to alarm you,' said Clarissa, 'but we think this man was coming in to kill you.'

Frank gazed eagerly around the bed to look down at who his apparent killer would be. He saw Hope lying on the ground as well. He looked up at Clarissa, giving a look of annoyance. 'That's Swen. Swen's not here to kill me.'

'How do you know?' asked Clarissa.

'Because I hired him. I hired him to protect me and find out what was going on. Swen's a contract killer. No better person here to protect you, find out what's going on. I don't come to places like this with nobody looking after me.'

'And me neither,' said Hope, looking up and giving Clarissa a smile. 'What did you hit him with?' she asked.

Clarissa looked down. 'About eight grands' worth of pottery. Oops.' She delicately placed the remains of the smashed vase back on the pedestal it had occupied on one side of the room. It was apparent to Hope that Macleod had been right. Clarissa from a distance had saved the day and Hope hadn't even heard her enter the room. A voice suddenly shouted through from outside.

'What the hell's going on? Who's there?'

'You can come in,' said Frank. 'It's all right. One of the officers has just smashed a pot over Swen's head.'

'Your Swen? I thought he was meant to be looking after you. Wasn't the old girl, was it? How on earth did he get trapped by the old girl?' Sarah marched in, straight into Clarissa, who was grinning.

'Nothing like us old girls,' she said. 'We can handle ourselves. You knew Swen was working for Frank?'

'Frank told me when we came down here. I was a little bit upset, so he said not to worry.'

'Swen was coming out to tell me what he'd found out,' said Frank. 'He was having to do it in the dark. He'd searched everywhere before.'

'Searched for what?' asked Hope.

'The knife. The knife that killed the Duke. The knife that may have killed Pavel.'

'And he didn't find anything, did he?' said Hope. 'I was watching him.'

'Well, he found you, but he decided not to say,' said Frank.

'You really need to be a bit quieter on the move. Trouble is, at the moment, Sergeant, we don't know what's going on. I'm worried I'm here to be framed. I'm worried I'm here to be the supposed person who took out the family. That's not a rap I want. Sure, things have been tough sometimes, working with the Zupcis, but I run my business with them and the Duke was always fairly reasonable. They've been good for business in a lot of ways. I certainly wouldn't want them as enemies. Brutal, brutal to the end. Especially back in their family history. The way they got to the top, you don't want to know.'

'I think I do,' said Hope.

'They certainly weren't shy about executing people. People out of line, people they needed gone because they were too good at putting up obstacles in their path. Politically corrupt with the underhand running of criminal business. They've got that newly fledged country in their hand, and yet when you worked with the Duke, you didn't see it,' said Frank.

'He's right,' said Sarah. 'He was just sex starved in a lot of ways or sex-crazed. That trait with his sons, that was him. I never saw him as a decision maker.'

'I always felt somebody was pulling his strings. Weird for a male-dominated country.'

'It's all wrong. There's somebody behind this,' said Sarah, 'and I'm worried. It was all right when we were talking movies. I didn't mind playing along with the Duke to get where I wanted to get. I wasn't going to get it through legitimate means, but he was good to me. Even when things weren't right, he always treated me well. Called it quits on the movies. I'm not even sure it was his decision, but when it happened, he looked after me, kept wanting to see me. Trouble is, if there's somebody behind him, I'm worried that . . . '

'What? Mischa?' asked Hope. 'You think she might be coming for you? But her family's being taken out.'

'Exactly,' said Sarah. 'I can't work out what's going on. I want out. I want away from here. It's not good.'

'No, it's not,' said Frank. 'I need off here, too. That's why Swen's here.'

'But Mischa invited him, didn't she, though? Or the Duke?'

'That's right, but once he was here, I bought him out. Realised he wasn't on a contract from them but just asked to be here.'

'Another suspect,' said Clarissa. 'A suspect brought in. Think about it. You all, all suspects, all people who could have done this. Why? Who's covering it up? Who's on top of this game?'

'I don't know and I don't care,' said Sarah. 'Just get me out of here soon.' With that, she walked out off to her own bedroom while Frank sat and looked down at Swen. 'Hopefully, he'll come around in a few minutes. I don't know if you want to be here, though, having clocked him.'

'He doesn't bother me. He's clearly not after us, and the last thing he's going to do is kill an officer in the UK. If he's a contract killer, he doesn't kill unless he has to.'

'True,' said Frank. 'But somebody is, and you better find out soon because this weather looks like it's set in for another couple of days. And a few of us might not be leaving.'

Chapter 18

Macleod sat in his room, a single candle still burning while he waited for his sergeants to return. In some ways, he was confused at Hope's desperateness to tail Swen down, but he knew in his own mind that Swen was a contract killer. He wasn't about to finish Hope off. The last thing he needed was to bring attention to himself by killing police officers on the island. If he was there for somebody else, he'd go and do that.

Hope at times was quick and too trusting in her own abilities. She always thought she could handle things in a physical sense, but Macleod always reckoned that it was best not to even contemplate those things. Better to stay clear at a distance, operate in a safer fashion, and he knew with Clarissa it would be like that. If Macleod had really thought Swen would act against the pair, he would never have sent them out, or at the very least, he would have followed them.

There came a rap at the door and Macleod thought it wasn't the sure knock of Hope's hand. Neither was it the rather belligerent way in which Clarissa knocked, as if she was disgusted the door hadn't opened for her on her arrival. Instead, this knock was delicate, almost alluring, if a knock could be that.

'Inspector,' said a whispered voice. 'Inspector, I need to talk to you.'

Macleod was in his pyjamas and had a small dressing gown with him, which he wrapped himself up in before opening the door. Lyla Preen stood there, still dressed as she had been for dinner with an off the shoulder dress that stopped just below the knees. Despite her age, she still looked an alluring woman and she smiled with a lipstick laden mouth at Macleod as she entered the room and closed the door gently behind her. She didn't remain at the door but instead sat down at the single seat in front of his dresser.

'I need some protection, Inspector.'

'With all due respect, Miss Preen, I think we all need protection at the moment.'

'I can't stay in my room, and I didn't want to go to the beach house. I don't trust Frank. Well, nobody trusts Frank, do they, with the way he is? And Sarah, she's not an operator. She doesn't know how to protect herself, just a big, dumb girl with goods the Duke liked. I need somebody smarter, someone to look after me at the moment. I think you might be that person.'

'With all due respect,' said Macleod, 'I'm here to look after everyone, but why would they want you? You were only in some films, as I understand it. Why would the killer come hunting someone for film work, even if the men liked you?'

'I wasn't just in films, Inspector,' said Lyla, standing up and walking over to him. 'You see, I was in other films as well.' She turned her head away as if these other films had winded her somehow.

'You can cut the theatrics,' said Macleod. 'Just tell me what happened.'

148

'I was promised a film role from Alexei. The Duke had put me onto him, but then they steered me towards a film for Victor. You saw how Victor died. You can imagine the film was not just raunchy, it was—'

'Erotic?' said Macleod.

'If only,' said Lyla, 'More explicit than erotic. I was younger then. Well, not that young.'

Macleod breathed a sigh of relief. He was wondering what age the woman was going back to for a moment. 'But I've been in the films for Victor, Alexei also, and the Duke. I had relations with him to get into the films and then he kept spending large amounts of money on me. I'm just worried that someone's decided that they've had enough of women playing around with their men.'

'So, what? You think Mischa's just killing off all the men? That's her husband and her sons.'

'Scorned, though, wasn't she? But why her? It could be Yulia. Yulia could be the one.'

'With all due respect,' said Macleod, 'I can't see Yulia carving up her slice of meat, never mind killing off several men. If I have to remind you, the Duke was naked and dumped in the sea. I don't see an older woman like Yulia Zupci being able to do that.'

'But she's got servants,' said Lyla.

For a moment, Macleod wondered if the woman was just simply being paranoid or if this actually was a reasonable explanation. The servants were not just servants. They were protection as well. Were they part and parcel of the Zupci crime family? Did they go and do the dirty work for them? Did Ivan sort it out for Yulia? Still, Macleod thought it unlikely that the old woman had been part of this.

'I don't think they'll just stop with the men. I think they'll come for us. Those here, those who play around. Myself, Sarah.'

'But why? Why bring everyone here and do this?' said Macleod. 'Surely they just could have bumped you off somewhere else. You wouldn't even know they'd done it.'

It suddenly hit him. This was a stage, wasn't it? This was a stage. Why was he here? To be part of the stage, part of theatrics, part of the show, and what was that show meant to be? Macleod took a walk over to the window, opened it and looked out into the dark, hoping to see his sergeants returning. He was uncomfortable with Lyla being here, for she said everything with such a quiet voice, one that soothed and reached into you. She was also an actress. Maybe she was trying to find out things from him, or maybe she was setting him up to ignore her. She'd been scorned by the Duke at the end, hadn't she?

'When the films all ended,' asked Macleod, 'how did you feel?'

He had his back to her and went to turn to have a look at her face for the answer, but a pair of hands were already on his shoulders.

'How do you think I felt? A little bit scorned, yes, Inspector, but I still receive things from them. Money. I'm still able to have a career of sorts. Not the one I would have had, not before the Duke was murdered, and Alexei. Karina, when she married Alexei, they hadn't known each other for very long. I think she was put in place after three or four months, and she's not Alexei's type. Alexei was much more like Victor, although without the total excess. Alexei was like his father, enjoyed women, enjoyed having them around. Karina, she's

150

stronger. American too, from the outside. Someone said she had connections to the underworld out there. I don't know if it's true, but I can imagine it.'

'Do you think Alexei loved her?' asked Macleod.

'Alexei would love anything in a dress, anything that would satisfy his ego and his other needs. One thing I'm capable of, and I think Karina is capable of, is satisfying men's needs.' Lyla's hands ran down the sides of Macleod's waist until they reached his hips. He could feel her pulling herself close up to him.

'You don't need to do that to gain my favour or trust,' said Macleod. 'I'm a police officer and a detective inspector. My job is to stop these murders, to keep other people alive as long as possible.'

He put his hands on her hands, took them off his hips and turned round and suddenly had Lyla's face in his. He took her shoulders, pushing her back gently.

'I'm not like the men of this family. I have a job to do, and I will do it.' He could smell her. Actually, he could smell her perfume. It was enticing and he knew that there was part of him that was seriously aroused by the woman. She could play all the cards, but he had someone at home who kept coming to mind and it was Jane.

'I have a partner at home who needs me,' said Macleod, 'and I need to get back there quickly, so I need to solve this, and I don't need you distracting me. It won't be long before my sergeants get back. I think you should stay over with Sergeant Urquhart in her room. You'll be safe there.'

'I feel far safer here, Inspector. After all, they're not going to go for you.'

'Why?' asked Macleod. 'Who knows who they'll go for?

151

Clarissa's got much more street savvy than I do.'

'I find that hard to believe, Inspector.' Once again, Lyla put her a hand up on Macleod's shoulder. 'Really, I think it best if I stay with you.'

There was a knock on the door. Before Macleod could say anything, the door was opened and Clarissa barged in.

'You're not going to believe this, Seoras, but . . . oh, hello?' said Clarissa. 'Sorry. I didn't realise you were interviewing.'

'Miss Preen is just feeling a little bit insecure at the moment. I have said that she can stop over in your room. You'd offer a level of protection that I couldn't.'

'Well, as long as it's only protection you need.'

Now Lyla kept her hand on Macleod's shoulder, and it moved across to his neck, gently stroking the back of it. Macleod put his hand up to try and remove it, but the woman kept it there and looked up at him. 'Thank you, Inspector, for everything.'

She reached up and gave him a kiss on the cheek before removing her hand, walking halfway across the room and then turning back.

'Where is your sergeant's room?' she said to Macleod, despite the fact Clarissa was standing beside her.

'Sergeant Urquhart will show you to that room very shortly. If you'd kindly stand outside for a moment, she needs to report to me.'

Lyla nodded and stepped outside while Macleod looked somewhat sheepishly down at the ground.

'I know a woman who's a player,' said Clarissa, 'and I know you. So, get over yourself. Listen. We tailed Swen out; he's working for Frank. He was going out there to tell him.'

'So, it's Frank?' queried Macleod. 'I knew there was somebody behind Swen. Hope described the other night how he was searching and searched just above her, had doubled back into the room. Yes. I knew he was working for someone. Why is he working for Frank?'

'Frank's worried that he is liable to be attacked or get fitted up for some of these murders. He didn't bring Swen with him. Swen was invited, but Frank knows him as a contract killer. He hired Swen to protect himself. Frank and Sarah are worried. Sarah's really panicked out there. I take it Miss Preen's the same?'

'Miss Preen has had some dubious dealings with this family, especially the menfolk. I think she must have bedded most of them. She's purporting the theory that some of the womenfolk are doing this, dispatching the men.'

'That doesn't seem to fit the bill,' said Clarissa. 'From what we understand, the Duke played around quite a bit. Victor did too, but then all of a sudden, they start dispatching them. Why didn't Mischa, Yulia, or whoever it is that's committing the murders polish off the Duke earlier? Why here with these people about?'

'Who knows? Maybe he felt safe,' said Macleod. 'We need to gather and talk this through. Maybe there's a thread we're not seeing. Maybe we're not understanding why. I just don't get it. Families like these, the idea that you go around and just start killing off the menfolk because they were playing around. They play around in lots of these types of criminal families. I thought it was expected. Sounds like it's a possible diversion from Frank.'

'Well, whatever it is, you're right, Seoras, we need to talk about it. Hope will be back shortly. She's just making sure Swen wakes up correctly.'

'Swen wakes up? What happened to him?'

'I broke an eight-thousand-pound vase over his head. It's all right. It's not the greatest piece of art I've broken in my lifetime.'

Macleod gave a little shake of his head. 'You better go and get Lyla secured in your room. I'll come and get you when Hope's back.'

'Okay,' said Clarissa, marching to the door. 'Don't worry, your secret's safe with me.' Macleod saw a wide grin as Clarissa left his room.

Chapter 19

Macleod knocked on Clarissa's door, and it was swiftly opened. He could see Lyla sitting inside at the far end of the bedroom on an upholstered chair. Clarissa raised her eyebrows as he walked in.

'You sure you want to do it here with her?' asked Clarissa.

'Yes,' said Macleod. 'I want to see just exactly who she is. No better way than getting her involved in the conversation.'

As Macleod walked further into the room, he saw Hope lying on the bed, leather jacket flung to one side, and he smiled as he saw her. When she'd gone off after Swen, Macleod had thought she'd be okay, thought that he'd guessed Swen correctly, but you never knew.

'Do you want to take top seat?' asked Clarissa, walking over to a tray of coffee and bringing one over to Macleod. Clarissa had a large flask of hot water supplied by Ivan, as all the guests did. He sat down in what was an elegant wooden chair at the top end of the room, glancing across at Lyla, who seemed to be fidgety.

'You okay, Miss Preen?' he asked. 'There's no need to be nervous now. You're in with us.'

'Forgive me, Inspector. Sorry. Forgive me, Seoras. It's just that I don't feel very safe with anyone at the moment. Not until we get out of here.'

'That's what we're here for,' said Macleod. 'To bash over some ideas about what's going on. So, let's do it.'

'Get some coffee in you first,' said Clarissa. 'You don't think well without coffee.'

'She's right there,' said Hope. 'Although she did say to me, you'd be right grouchy without it as well.'

Macleod fired a look over at Hope and nodded almost imperceptibly in the direction of Lyla Preen. Hope turned her mouth down, indicating that she didn't think Miss Preen was that genuine.

'Okay, let's bring our thoughts together. This idea of female revenge we've been knocking about; frankly, the men in this family are far from perfect.'

'They're randy perverts,' said Clarissa.

'Certainly playing the field,' said Hope.

'They do like their women,' said Lyla Preen. 'The women do like them, to be fair. I do know that.'

'Do you? Or were you just trying to get somewhere in your career?' asked Macleod.

'It's a little bit of both, Inspector. These men have power. They all have power. It's quite the aphrodisiac.'

'I remember when an aphrodisiac was a couple of nips of whisky behind the bike shed and . . . '

'That's enough, Sergeant,' said Macleod to Clarissa. 'Let's keep our train of thought. If, as we say, the menfolk are being punished for not behaving correctly, not being faithful, the obvious person would be Mischa.'

'Not necessarily,' said Hope. 'There's Mischa and there's Yulia.'

156

'And there's always those they've slighted,' said Clarissa, looking over at Lyla Preen.

'Yes,' she said. 'I could see why Sarah would be capable.'

Clarissa looked back at Macleod. Because Lyla couldn't see her face, she raised her eyebrows towards Macleod, indicating the richness of the statement that had just been made.

'Let's focus on the family,' said Macleod. 'Mischa. Now Mischa could do it. After all, she's running this household. She said about her husband that he'd gone out. She was in the bedroom, so she's got no alibi for that. And with Pavel, like the rest of us, she was off getting ready.'

'No, she wasn't,' said Lyla. 'She wasn't. I didn't like to say, but I'd had a confrontation with her. She'd been down getting everything ready, and I'd just come from a little exercise with Julie McGeehan. Mischa had wanted to speak to me, talk to me about the films. One in particular that she was worried would get out, was going to sully the reputation of one of the companies that have produced the film. It was one of those films with Victor. Anyway, we weren't ready for dinner, and she said she was in a hurry, so we did what good ladies do. She came to my room, I got changed, I went to hers and she got changed.'

'You didn't think to mention this to us?' asked Macleod.

'I didn't want it being common knowledge. It was business dealings. At the time, Alexei probably would have got annoyed. He deals with all of that.'

'In the midst of all this, as Mischa is still dealing with the family issues,' said Hope, 'she's still running businesses; she's still looking towards that.'

'Of course. Families like this don't run on sentiment,' said Lyla. 'Why do you think I'm here? I've obviously been brought here for that reason, to talk on the quiet about business dealings I've had with them. I wouldn't be surprised if some of the others have been asked the same. I didn't tell you because other people would find out. We keep all this business quiet. It's all done off the record, especially if we're sounding things out first of all.'

'She'd just lost her husband and her son. Maybe about to lose a second son,' replied Clarissa.

'I can tell you it wasn't her. She's their mum, anyway. I could see myself killing a husband but would you really kill your own children?' asked Lyla.

Macleod sat in thought. He had no children of his own. He looked over towards Hope, who had no children either. Neither had Clarissa. In fact, of the team, the only person thinking about possibly having children was Ross. Well, he'd mentioned it to Macleod, asking for his opinion on just how a child would affect being available for investigations. Macleod didn't have a clue about that. Could a mother break that bond? Could she?

'So, if Mischa was with you, that rules that out. Maybe look at somebody else.'

'Yulia?' said Clarissa. 'You can't seriously tell me you think that old biddy did it. She barely speaks English and there's two people with her when she comes to talk to anyone. Not really the type for a murderer, is she, Seoras?'

'Well, I don't know. What do you think, Miss Preen?'

Lyla looked somewhat shocked. 'She's an octogenarian! She was a serious piece of work back in the old days. They say she built up this family, but Clarissa is right. How on earth could she actually carry these things out?'

'Maybe she didn't,' said Hope. 'Maybe she ordered them.'

'She's not head of the family; she hasn't got the power to do that. Hasn't got the right. You don't step in front of the others running the family.'

'So, Alexei would get the final say on that?' asked Hope

'If they were taking people out, yes.'

'What about the idea that Swen could be doing it for her?' said Macleod.

'Swen's working for Frank.'

'Or maybe Frank thinks Swen's working for him,' said Hope. 'Maybe it's all just . . . '

Macleod stood up, he turned and began to pace the room. 'It's too much, isn't it? Too much. Normally you can see the decent person amongst it all. You can spot the one who's innocent, but here, everyone, just everyone's got something. You couldn't rule anyone out.'

'Well, thank you,' said Lyla Preen. 'That's a real vote of confidence.'

'Oh, come on, Miss Preen. Let's be honest here; you'd do anything to get yourself ahead in your industry. My goodness, you sold your body to men just to get into films.'

The woman looked back at him coldly. 'Sarah is the one who would do that,' she said. 'She was the one in the magazines; she was the one who would sell anything she had. I was a film star being loved.'

'Tell yourself that,' said Macleod. 'Tell yourself that,' and he turned away, shaking his head.

'What about Kira, Seoras?' asked Hope.

'She's quite young for it, though, isn't she?'

'But not incapable,' said Hope. 'She's a slight figure in some senses.'

'But, Seoras,' said Clarissa, 'she has to kill her father and her

159

brothers. It's not easy. That's quite detached.'

'It's not her. It's not Kira,' said Lyla. 'She was with me.'

'What do you mean she was with you?' said Macleod. 'Did you tell us anything? Your reliability gets lower and lower every time you open your mouth.'

'No, she was with me. She was setting up my meeting with Mischa. It was when Victor died. We were meeting on the quiet, out of the way. Can't be her. She had brought documents and things for me to read, and she took them away with her so they would never exist if I turned everything down.'

'And did you?'

'No, I was for accepting. That's the whole point. That's why I want to get out of here. I've made peace with them. Whoever is doing this killing, I want to get out of the way. For what it's worth, I think it's Sarah. That's why she's off with Frank now. She'll probably bump him off next.'

'Why Frank?' asked Macleod.

'Frank was one of the ones who introduced her to the family, to the Duke, before the Duke got all close with her. The Duke promised her a lot of things that never came true. I told you she's the one who'd prostitute herself for anything, but now she hasn't got her share. Swen's probably working for her.'

'Well, if Swen is working for her,' said Hope, 'he's running a very good act. Frank and Swen gave a very convincing line about working together.'

'Maybe they did,' said Macleod, 'but Swen could be working for somebody else, just letting Frank believe that he's with him. It's good cover. If Lyla's right, then Sarah's got Frank where she wants him.'

'Except it's a rubbish thing to do. She's the only one down with him, it'd give her away in an instant. And more than that said Clarissa. 'You've got to think about who could be culpable here. You've got to think who's actually going to pay for the crime.'

'What do you mean?' asked Lyla.

'Well, here you're on what's technically embassy soil. We weren't sent in in our full capacity. We were told to come in and investigate as a favour.'

'So, what, you can't actually arrest anyone?'

'So, it would seem,' said Macleod. 'I was invited here by Mischa to find her husband's killer.'

'So where are we at?' asked Clarissa. 'Because, from my own understanding, it can't be Mischa, at least for one of the deaths. It can't be Kira for the other. Yulia's too weak and frail. Sarah, according to Miss Preen here, is capable of it, but I'm not seeing any other follow-through of that, and then you've got yourself, Miss Preen, come to us looking for help. I take it Mischa and Kira will back you up on the fact you were with them looking at contracts and talking about the issues around the films.'

'Of course, they won't,' said Lyla. 'They're not going to admit to doing deals like that. You don't have a family like this losing face in that way.'

'We haven't even got to the men yet,' said Macleod.

'We're running out of them,' said Clarissa, and received a look from Macleod.

'Alexei could be taking over,' said Hope.

'But once his father was gone, he did take over. Pavel's not going to take over from him. He's not going to come after him. Victor was a stoned druggie,' said Macleod. 'Why would he be bothered about running anything? It doesn't make sense for the brothers to be killed off afterwards. I can see why Alexei

161

would kill his father, but not beyond that.'

'What about Frank, then? Maybe Frank is leading Swen down the line and bumping them all off.'

'I haven't ruled Frank out,' said Macleod, 'but it's an awfully brave move on this piece of ground. Surely there'd be better places for him to do that.'

Silence filled the room and Clarissa roared an almighty yawn. 'I'm tired,' she said. 'This is getting us nowhere. Why don't we get to bed?'

Macleod reached down and grabbed the drink he was cupping and sipped it. 'Fresh start in the morning, then. Take care of Miss Preen,' he said to Clarissa.

'It's clear that you don't think it's me,' said Lyla Preen. 'Leaving me with your sergeant.'

'I didn't say that.' Macleod turned for the door, looking at Hope. 'Are you coming, McGrath?'

'But you're leaving me with her. So, you're obviously quite happy. Nobody else is staying in this room, so you mustn't think it's me,' said Lyla.

'I'm leaving you with the one person I think wouldn't hesitate, if you came anywhere near her, to strike back with full force or who will strike out at anyone coming in through that door. Trust me, Miss Preen, you've been ruled out of nothing.'

Macleod turned away, opened the door, and walked out into the corridor, followed by Hope. 'Goodnight, Sergeant,' he said over his shoulder and heard Clarissa say goodnight from the door before closing it.

'You learn anything from that?' asked Hope.

'Yes, I did. I think she's telling the truth. I think she is very genuine. Otherwise, what's the point? Why get Mischa and

Kira off the hook? These people aren't best buddies. There's nothing, no good in it. She wants to know who the murderer is. She's genuinely worried.'

'So, who's your money on?'

'I don't know, because Mischa was my prime suspect, and Lyla's just blown that out of the water.'

Chapter 20

Macleod could feel the rattle on the windows when he woke up and pulled the covers over his head for a moment. He wanted to think. He wanted to blow away the cobwebs that were clouding this case, but he couldn't. Had to be Mischa. It had to be. Everything pointed that way and yet Lyla, she wasn't lying.

Well, why was she killing her sons? thought Macleod. That was the other problem he had. He had to work out why this woman, who was clearly distressed when she saw Pavel's dead body, was killing her sons. Was Swen being put up to it? Was it one of the many servants? Were they working it that way?

Clearly, the menfolk had been misbehaving, but it was quite a brutal way to deal with it. Should she have called her husband in, explained to him? Or maybe it was seen as being okay. Maybe that was the problem. There was no way to pull him back in.

Couldn't she have had her own man, though? That was one of the things Macleod was having difficulties with, putting himself in their place. The whole debauchery of it, especially amongst a family. He'd seen in many gangs where people were betrayed by other people. They'd gone off, done things they shouldn't have before the boss man had said so, and they paid for it with their lives. Those climbing the ranks had taken away those above them, but they weren't parents and children.

He could have understood if the guests had been the ones being bumped off, but also why was he here? Why would you invite somebody like him if you were trying to do away with your family and not get caught? It was all getting too much for him, and he realised there was a fog across his mind and that fog was his worry for Jane.

He hadn't been able to speak to her in the last couple of days. Maybe she'd be getting worried as well. She did. She fretted over him. He knew that, but he also knew that she was the first one to send him out to these cases. Back home, she'd be trying to stand on her own or at least with Angus's help. She would want to be strong for him, want to be able to let him do what he was made to do in his own life, to be this detective that the media thought he was.

Macleod rolled out of bed, stumbled over to put on the shirt and tie he'd worn yesterday. He hadn't that many with him, just a couple. Rather than any of the staff wash them, he continued to wear them. Besides, there was no power and he wasn't going to make somebody wash everything of his by hand. He wasn't Clarissa.

It would also give them a reason for having access to his room if the servant needed to drop the clothes back off. He made it clear that his room was to be untouched and not entered. Ivan had been told so, and as far as he could tell, it hadn't been entered at all.

Having dressed, he crossed the corridor to Hope's room to find her already up, wearing yesterday's t-shirt and jeans.

'You look like you haven't slept,' said Hope.

'Well, thank you for that,' said Macleod. 'That's uplifting.'

'What do you want me to say? Morning, gorgeous?' Macleod turned and gave a frown to Hope. 'You're right,' she said. 'It's more Clarissa.'

Macleod picked up his weary feet, walked over to Clarissa's room and knocked the door. It opened and Clarissa's smiling face looked back at Macleod. 'Well, good morning, gorgeous Oh, you look fine.'

Macleod raised a finger towards Hope before she could say anything. 'Are you ready, Sergeant?' he said. 'I take it Miss Preen is coming with us.'

'Absolutely. Chatterbox of the year,' said Clarissa.

'You don't have to speak like that in front of her,' said Macleod.

'She's in the bathroom. She'll be two minutes. But I'll tell you something, Seoras. I think she's telling the truth. She is scared. Really scared. I'm not sure she slept a wink.'

'Did you?'

'Well, you know that sleep we do?'

'The one where you don't?' said Macleod.

'That's the one.'

'Find the older I get, the less sleep I need anyway. I'm sure you're the same.'

'Well, thanks,' said Clarissa. 'Thank you for that. You know how to lift a woman up, don't you?'

Macleod told Clarissa to follow down with Lyla Preen, and together with Hope, he descended the stairs to the large dining room at the bottom of the house. The double doors were opened. As he stepped inside, he saw that Mischa was already there, Alexei hadn't arrived yet, Frank and Sarah were missing, but Swen was sitting at the end of the table with some eggs and toast.

'We've got some gas stoves,' said Mischa. 'So, we can do some hot food if you want it. The man at the end there can make a mean omelette.'

Macleod looked over at one of the servants. He gave a muted smile.

'That would be absolutely splendid,' said Macleod. 'Hope?' Hope nodded behind him. 'Two omelettes then. Just put whatever in them. Surprise me.'

Macleod heard the snicker from Hope when he said this, and he realised it was quite out of character for him. That was the trouble at the moment. The whole case was out of character. The whole case was not formalised. It wasn't even a case.

Yulia was at the table, not at the head with Mischa, but to one side. The woman was still dressed in black, the only person in the household who still was, but it seemed that Mischa had decided not to bother this time. Pavel was dead, Victor was dead, and her husband, the Duke, was dead. Mischa had every reason to still be in black, but he thought that Yulia looked dignified, if nothing else.

Sitting down to the omelette, Macleod tucked into it heartily and when coffee was placed in front of him, he smiled. If they were trying to use him and manipulate him, they certainly knew how to go about it with food and coffee.

'I'm afraid we're going to have to start searching rooms. We have got no physical evidence,' he said to Mischa. 'There's a murder weapon out there. One I need to find, one which the killer will be hiding if they haven't thrown it away somewhere out into the sea. It'll be of use. We can at least trace where it came from. We may even get fingerprints on it and besides that, I think a search of rooms would be important anyway. It may bring a lot more evidence to light.'

'No,' said Mischa.

'Excuse me?' said Macleod. 'The least you can do is let me search Pavel's room properly. And your husband's. I take it you have different rooms at times. You may not have always slept together?'

Mischa raised her eyes at him. 'He had work rooms and such, yes.'

'Of course. I think I should search those, and those of Victor. Search them fully.'

'Next you'll be telling me you want your forensics in these rooms when they arrive.'

'Of course,' said Macleod.

Mischa was wearing a pair of black leather trousers and a crimson shirt. Macleod thought she looked like she was off to a day in the office. She stood up abruptly, spun around behind her chair and looked down at Macleod. 'No. We have guests here. They need to be afforded their privacy in a time of mourning. Yulia has lost her son and her grandsons. I have lost my boys. At this time, we don't want to be disturbed with your searches. Can you not do your work without this constant drive to procedure? I brought you here because I thought you were more of a brain than a numbers man. More than someone who just trawled along.'

'You know nothing about being a police officer then,' said Macleod. 'Ninety percent of what we come up with is because we trawl. We're like a fishing boat. You put the net out and you pull on. Sure, sometimes you snag the wrong thing. You catch the wrong fish, and you throw it back. Eventually, you get what you want. Sometimes it's a big hole. We don't sit down detecting all day. We muddy the water; we stir it up and see what floats to the top. That's why I need to do physical searches. I need to upset people.'

'Well, not now,' said Mischa. 'At this time, the guests deserve their privacy. But more than that, those not with us deserve it. You'll go in and you'll dig up the muck and the...,—who knows what of their private habits? I'm not having it. Pavel wasn't perfect, but I'm not going to have you go in and destroy his name.'

'Pavel obviously was quite challenged when it came to intimacy with women,' said Macleod. 'These things don't bother me. I will be looking. I will trawl and I'm going to muddy the waters.'

'Well, don't,' said Mischa. 'Just get on with it.'

She turned on her heel and marched out of the room. As Macleod looked across the table, Yulia was looking back at him sternly. He didn't say anything, but Macleod could feel the coldness. Picking up his coffee, he excused himself to McGrath and walked to the end of the table where Swen was continuing his breakfast with some muesli and milk. Macleod sat down beside him, a cup in hand, leaned over quietly, saying, 'I believe you were speaking with my sergeant last night.'

'Yes,' said Swen. 'Both of them.'

'You're working for Frank, keeping him safe.'

'That is correct, Inspector.'

'Well, then, maybe you can help me keep him safe. At the moment, it seems like the men of the family are the ones in trouble. Only the menfolk are being dispatched. How would you do it, Swen? I know who you are. I know what you do. So how would you do it?'

'Maybe you'd wait until they were all getting together and plant a bomb,' he said. 'Or wait until they were on a retreat

169

away from a lot of other people, walk in, shoot them all dead,' he said. 'This is rather protracted. It's not the way I would do it if I was paid to. You see, Inspector, what's being done here is a point is being made of some sort. Can you feel the tension? I believe that you were speaking to Mischa about searching the rooms. You weren't exactly quiet, so forgive me, but I can lipread well, and she's blocked you from doing it. Well, I will be searching the rooms for Frank. He's asked me to. Frank is worried, very worried. Something's afoot with the family, he says, and he's worried that he will take the blame. I will make sure that doesn't happen.'

'You understand these people better than I do,' said Macleod. 'You're hired by them; you work for them. Would they kill family?'

'That's an awkward question, Inspector. Would they move family out of the way? Well, yes, it's happened many a time within organised crime. The said family member was well out of line, having done something particularly heinous. Usually it would be done quietly, discreetly. The outside world might not even know it. This is a pointless statement. The world would know that they've been murdered.'

'Why am I here?' asked Macleod. 'Why would I be brought into the fray if the family was doing it?'

'I specialise with a gun. I make people disappear. I end people. Trying to understand how these other people work, trying to fathom their real reasons is beyond me. I just take the money.'

Macleod nodded and sat back in his chair. He didn't think he could ever be as cold as Swen. Sitting beside him, he truly detested the man. To kill somebody just for money, that seemed to Macleod to be the worst. To kill from anger, to kill

170

rom vengeance, from emotions stirred up that you could not control seemed so much more forgivable than simply taking money to kill someone. But if Swen was going to search the rooms, Macleod would find out what he discovered. Macleod turned back to Swen.

'I know you've already tried the eggs, but you should try an omelette. He really does make a very good omelette.'

'You can only break so many eggs in a day, Inspector. At least that's what I've found.'

Chapter 21

larissa encouraged Lyla down the stairs, trying not to hurry but instead maintain a dignified pace. Clarissa wasn't used to hurrying, but the woman had taken so long to get ready, she wondered if Macleod would still be there. She could imagine the scowl she would get from him arriving so late. In fact, she wondered if breakfast was still being served. Surely, they would, considering other guests hadn't arrived. She listened to the wind outside as they descended the stairs, howling round the house. As large as it was, it was still no match for the Hebridean storms that came at it. The hallway was lit with the occasional candle making the wind seem even more dramatic. When they reached the large dining room on the ground floor, Clarissa realised that she, too, was starving.

On entering the dining room, Clarissa watched Lyla take up a seat on her own in the middle of the table. A servant attended her, and she almost gave Clarissa the brush off for sitting beside her. Highly indignant, thought Clarissa, considering the fact she's kept me waiting all this time.

Still, she looked over and saw the man at the end of the table with a small gas pan and a number of eggs beside him. She ordered a large three egg omelette and looked around for somewhere to sit. Clearly Lyla didn't want her sitting with her. Swen was on his own at the end of the table. It looked like he'd almost finished, while at the top, Mischa's seat was empty, but Yulia was sitting across from it. Clarissa made her way to sit two seats down from Yulia. The woman was the oldest member of the family and something in Clarissa didn't want to disturb her unless the woman asked to speak to her. Besides, she barely spoke English, so what was the point?

Sitting this close to the splendour of the family made Clarissa feel better. Unlike Macleod, Clarissa was at ease in a house like this. Every time she moved from room to room, she saw some piece of artwork that spoke to her. They were lost on Macleod. Not just the monetary value of them, but how evocative the many pieces were, how they seemed to bring to life such subjects that she never got to speak about with the team.

Clarissa could imagine herself in a house like this. She'd investigated many more similar to it, and there was something comforting about it, despite the fact it had a large number of dead bodies within. There was an aristocracy within the building, something that spoke to Clarissa's soul, a family that had depth to them, a history behind them. She thought that maybe Macleod didn't get that.

Once her eggs had arrived, Clarissa tucked into the omelette, enjoying it with a large splash of coffee, Macleod's favourite brew. After she'd finished, she sat back for a moment, closing her eyes and a servant walked behind her towards Yulia. There was then a very quiet conversation. At first, she tuned out, thinking the conversation would be in Russian, not one of her strongest languages. When she heard whispering in English, and fluent, quick English, she became more interested in what was happening.

The conversation was quite banal. It mentioned clothing, what things were being washed and brought back up to Yulia and when she would be attended to throughout the day. Nothing that related to the case, but more to the old woman's habits. However, once she heard the conversation stop, Clarissa opened her eyes. Spotting the servant walk behind her, she raised her hand, calling her over.

'Forgive me, but do you speak English?'

'Yes,' said the young girl. 'I do. I speak it very well. I'm from here.'

'What, from Barra?' asked Clarissa.

'Yes, I work over here. Normally it's a couple of days at a time. I look after Madam Yulia, attending to her clothing and things. I'm just helping out in the dining room as well today.'

'Due to the power cut and that?'

'Absolutely. We're all a little bit under the pressure, and then, of course, with the other things that have been happening.'

'Of course. Tell me, does Madam Yulia speak English?'

'Yes. She normally speaks in Russian, but I don't have any Russian. They needed extra staff, so they took on some of us from the local area. They pay well. You don't ask many questions about what goes on. I mean, I shouldn't really say this.'

'It's okay,' said Clarissa. 'You can tell me. I won't feed any of it back.'

'Well, Victor, I had to do some errands around his rooms and that. The things you see. Crazy. Just crazy. You don't see those sorts of things on our island.'

'I've been trying to see some of those things all my life,' said Clarissa. 'Never got into that situation.' The girl went to laugh and then put her hand over her mouth.

'Are you okay?' said Clarissa.

'We're not meant to fraternise. You've asked a question, but I shouldn't be seen laughing with you. Frowned upon by the family. We're here to serve. Don't get me wrong; they treat us very well, but we're here to serve.'

'I won't get you into any more trouble,' said Clarissa.

She watched as the girl ran off and disappeared from the room. Beside Clarissa, Madam Yulia continued to sit at the table, a lone cup of coffee in front of her. Clarissa turned and looked at her. The woman looked back, giving a very brief smile before staring straight ahead again. *Why doesn't she go elsewhere?* thought Clarissa. *Or is she watching us? Maybe she's here to keep an eye on what's going on. Maybe the old woman's not as decrepit as she looks or how they make her out to be.*

Clarissa had an idea, picked up her cup and stepped past the two chairs that led to Yulia. She paused for a moment, leaning down briefly. 'Do you mind if I sit beside you? I'd like to ask you some questions.'

The woman turned and looked up at her and said something in Russian.

'If you're going to keep up that pretence,' said Clarissa, 'you really need to do it in a much quieter voice. I heard you talking to the servant. She doesn't speak any Russian and you speak very good English. May I take a seat beside you?'

The old woman smiled, held her hand out, indicating that Clarissa should take up the seat next to her.

'You don't look like your inspector,' said Yulia, 'but you are quite perceptive.'

'You look like a little old woman, but I fear you've got a lot more behind you than that.'

175

'Like I said, you're very perceptive.'

'Thank you. I'm sorry for your loss. It must be hard with so many people around as well,' said Clarissa.

'We have to maintain our standards, maintain our front. Some of our guests, they are not friends, they are business acquaintances. Would not be good to look weak in their sight.'

'How long has your family been established?' asked Clarissa. 'You have quite considerable wealth. I know that from the items I see around me. My boss wouldn't have a clue what he's looking at, but can I tell you something?'

The old lady nodded.

'If you look at the Monet in the far corner of the dining hall, that's a fake. I saw it yesterday. Most of your artwork isn't, but that one is.'

The old woman looked at her, narrowing her eyes. 'My son bought that.'

'Well, he should have had somebody with him who knew about art. It's distinctly a fake.'

'You're right, and he would have had if he'd listened. That's the trouble nowadays. The old ways, they don't follow them. We had people we kept close to us, people who could advise us on such things. How did you educate yourself in the arts? I thought it may be a fake; I didn't know. How do you know?'

'I used to be in the arts side, looking into stolen property, forgeries making their way into museums and family homes, working alongside insurance people. If I'm honest, it's not even a good fake.'

'It was never his strong point. Mischa was strong. Mischa helped him, Mischa bore him four children, including three sons. Sometimes you have to organise who is around them. Sometimes you have to take charge.'

'Is that what's happening here? Someone's taking charge?'

The woman reached down and picked up her coffee, sipping it slowly before putting it down. Clarissa thought she was almost chewing on it.

'I said you were perceptive,' said Yulia. 'Maybe you need to look with wider eyes.'

Clarissa could feel the door shutting but she didn't want the conversation to end.

'How did you get to rule over Zupci, to get it to break away? How was it done?'

'My husband laid the foundations of it, like his father had done beforehand, and we built up region by region. People knew and respected our name. They feared us, but they also knew they could trust us if they were close to us, if they were loyal.'

'Built on the name,' said Clarissa.

'Built on the family name. That's the thing, isn't it? The name can mean so much to people, even when they don't know the people at the top. We knew how to make a deal. Those on the outside coming in, looking for something from us. Well, we knew what we wanted from them, and we got it, and they didn't back down once we made a deal. We didn't entice them; we just put our terms out in front of them. People wanted to be dealing with us because we were strong. They knew nobody else would come in. That's what it's like in the country. People will take their lot as long as it's a reasonably happy lot. They don't want everything. They don't need everything; they need a bit of security, but to do that the name has to be there. The one they cling to, the one they support. But the family will go on despite my son's death. Despite the death of two of his sons. What did you think of the sons, if I may ask?'

'Your grandchildren were certainly different.'

'Victor took the worst of his father; he had no strong woman with him. Alexei was off on those paths, but Karina, she is his strength. That's what he says.'

'You found Victor to be what, a disappointment?'

'A disease. He was a disease. What kind of a person behaves like that? Makes it so well known?'

'And Pavel?'

'Pavel was ill. Weak. Couldn't control his mind. He was like a child, the way he ran after the staff. The family has to be strong. They needed to learn. Mischa had so much on her plate. So much to do with all of them. She understood at first. She was part of us, and she understood it was about the family. The family will go on.'

'I think I begin to see,' said Clarissa. 'And Alexei, he will uphold the family? He'll maintain it?'

The old woman looked straight ahead, then she sipped her coffee again. 'The requirement of duty. The family must be maintained.'

'Alexei will do that?' asked Clarissa again.

'That's why Karina was brought in. You don't marry for love in this family. Bring in someone strong to be alongside. You have to be part of the family.'

'And Karina is part of the family?'

'Alexei will always be part of the family,' said Yulia. 'But with strong people come strong desires. If you'll excuse me,' said the old woman, and put her hand up.

Two servants instantly arrived beside her and gave her a stick and escorted her from the room. On the way out, the old woman shrugged them off and walked over to the painting that Clarissa pointed out earlier. Without warning she grabbed it taking two tugs to pull it off the wall. She threw it onto the ground with a fierceness that surprised Clarissa. The frame broke and she kicked it away.

It was a futile gesture if she was looking to do more damage to the painting, but as it slid across, the action told Clarissa an awful lot about the woman. The old lady turned around, walked towards the door but stopped just as she reached it and shot a glance towards Clarissa. 'Yes,' she said, 'he should have spotted that was a fake.'

Chapter 22

Macleod spent the morning cruising amongst the guests. Frank and Sarah had joined from the beach house briefly, and only when the crowd had gathered in the gym hall at the rear of the house. Mischa was operating some card tables and drinks, keeping the party going, as she said it, entertaining her guests. Macleod thought it would be the perfect chance to get a look around rooms, but once again, Mischa denied him. It was awkward for Macleod because he was aware that she could refuse him access to the island, given his government's position. He had no authority to barge into rooms and he was feeling constantly frustrated with what he was doing, or rather, not getting to do.

At approximately twelve, everyone was sent to their rooms, told to freshen up and dress while the servants prepared lunch. Macleod watched Sarah and Frank return to the beach house, while Swen and Lyla stayed at the house. Macleod was watching carefully to see if Swen would make a dash to look around rooms, but he disappeared upstairs along with the general kerfuffle of everyone going to dress for lunch.

Every conversation that morning was short, suspicious. People were talking about nothing of note. With the number of deaths that had occurred, maybe they were scared to say anything. Whatever the reason, it wasn't getting Macleod any closer to the killer. He had lots of theories. Most of them seem to linger around the women of the family sorting out the menfolk. As he went up the stairs, Clarissa stopped him.

'An interesting thing I found out this morning,' she said, 'is that Yulia speaks English. She's very much from the family. Always the family and what the family do. We've got to start thinking about this place as an institution, not as a family. It's hard to imagine someone killing someone within their own family, even for the offense it could cause. The idea that Mischa would take out her own. You need to look at this as an institution, more like a mafia. In that way, I think we might get to the bottom of it.'

'I don't think we'll solve it,' said Macleod suddenly. 'I think we're being played. I think the final steps are coming up soon. We'll see what we can do at lunch.'

'What do you mean?' asked Clarissa.

'If I just wander around here, all that's going to happen is whatever plot we've been called into is going to take place. When we bring everyone to lunch. I think I'll stir the water. I'll muddy it. I'll declare someone as our killer.'

'In order to do what?'

'Didn't you hear me? Stir the water,' said Macleod.

'And if you're right?'

'If I'm right, nothing will happen because I believe that Mischa is behind this.'

'But they're not going to arrest themselves, are they? They're not going to hand themselves over, either.'

'They're going to use diplomatic immunity in everything they do, everything that's going on here,' said Macleod. 'I mean, the idea that our government would send me down here unless there was something they desperately needed from the Zupcis. I think it's time to stop playing. It's time to start doing.'

Macleod made it up to his own room, got changed and was awaiting the one o'clock time slot for lunch. He could go down earlier, but no one would be about and Macleod had had enough of talking to the servants. This was being operated at a higher level than them. Just before one o'clock, Macleod left his room, rapped on Hope's door before rapping Clarissa's as well. Lyla Preen was still with Clarissa, and together with the three women, Macleod strode down the stairs with purpose. He had expected everyone else to be leaving the rooms at that time and was surprised when he saw no one. Maybe he was a touch late, or maybe even a touch early. On arriving at the large hall for lunch, a servant opened the double doors. Macleod found an empty room.

'Where's Madame Mischa?' he asked the servant.

'Not here yet, nor Madame Yulia. We've not been called for.'

Macleod found this unusual, for Mischa had been early for every meal, there to greet her guests. After all, that's exactly what she'd been doing the whole time. Carrying on as if the guests were the important thing. Macleod sat down and was brought a cup of coffee.

'Seems a bit unusual, doesn't it?' queried Lyla. 'I mean, you'd expect them to be here, wouldn't you? I'd be on time. I wouldn't be one left on my own. Left behind with a killer on the loose.'

Macleod called over to one of the servants. 'Aren't you going to find out where Madame Mischa is? Tell her that some of her guests have arrived already for lunch. She wouldn't want to be caught out like that.'

The servant nodded and disappeared out of the room. He returned some five minutes later, looking flustered.

'I'm begging your pardon, Inspector. I can't find Madame Mischa. I can't find Madame Yulia either or Madame Kira.'

'Go and knock the door of the guests. See if they're there. See if Mr Drummond is ready,' said Macleod.

'I shall do, but Mr Schmidt and Miss Kurtz are out at the beach house. I'd rather not go that way in this wind. It could take a little while.'

'That's okay. Find Drummond first of all.' Macleod stood up from his chair. 'In fact, Hope, Clarissa, go and join them. Search this place. See if anyone's about.' Macleod watched his sergeants disappear and began pacing around the room.

'What's up?' asked Lyla. 'You think somebody's . . . ?'

'Somebody's played their hand already. Too late,' he whispered under his breath. It took Clarissa and Hope another five minutes before they returned to the dining room.

'Nobody about, Seoras. Absolutely nobody. It looks like everyone's out of the house except us. Julie McGeehan's here, but she's down with the servants eating with them in their quarters.'

'Well, if the house is empty,' said Macleod. 'We need to go outside, all three of us.'

Clarissa looked outside, saw the driving rain, the dark grey clouds. 'It's going to be bitter out there,' she said, turned around and grabbed her shawl that she had brought down with her, flinging it around her.

'Get geared up,' said Macleod. 'It's time to go. Miss Preen. You're welcome to stay with the servants or you can come with us.'

Macleod saw the worry on the woman's face. 'I'll go with

Clarissa. I'll stay close to her.'

'Okay,' said Macleod. 'I'll start off towards the beach house see if we can locate Frank and Sarah.'

As he stepped outside the house, he turned to Hope. 'No one is here, not even Madame Yulia. How does Yulia get about?'

'Clarissa did tell you she spoke English. Maybe she's got an act. Maybe she's livelier than she shows.'

'You could be right,' said Macleod. 'Blast it. Had the rug pulled out from under me. I was going to stir up the water. I was going to announce a killer. Come on, to the beach house'

Together the small party of four made the way out into the wild. Macleod felt the rain drive against his face. It wasn't particularly cold, but beneath his feet the ground was wet, and he could feel his shoes becoming sodden. He marched forward Hope stopped him.

'Look, Seoras, over there.' Macleod peered into the distance over towards the cliffs. At the edge of the small island, he could see what looked like a figure.

'Clarissa, continue to the beach house. If you get there and nobody's there, remain there. Stay well hidden. Lyla, you go with her. Come on, Hope. Let's find out who that is.'

Together the pair walked sideways into the wind as it drove them back away from the cliff. Macleod walked in the lee of Hope, her taller-framed figure helping to keep some of the wind off. She was also significantly fitter, and Macleod was glad of the shelter that came from his tall sergeant.

'We'd best be careful if this is Swen,' said Hope.

Around the island, a haar had started to form that would impede any vessels beyond the island from seeing the landmass As they got closer to the cliffs, however, Macleod could see that the water was still so rough he doubted if any boat would be coming soon. As they approached the cliff, the figure they had seen was gone. Macleod urged caution as they got closer.

'Just be careful where we go. You could get shoved over here in no time. Keep a small distance between us and our wits about us.'

'Always, Seoras, always,' said Hope. 'But if we're going to get to them before this killer does, we need to move.'

At the top of the cliff, Macleod looked down as the swell of the sea bounced off the rocks throwing white spray up high. The land was drenched anyway from the driving rain and the cliffs looked wet and slippery. As he surveyed the land around him, Macleod could see something in the water.

'There, Hope. What's that?'

'Bodies, people,' said Hope and began to clamber down the rocks.

'Easy,' shouted Macleod, but Hope was away. He understood her zeal. If there was a chance of rescuing someone, Hope would be there. Numerous times before she'd dived into water to save people, something that Macleod admired about her. Not just her desire to do it, but her strength and determination in making it happen.

Macleod picked his way down the rocks slowly, but they were slippery, and his shoes were not the best fit for clambering over a wet rock. He was also looking around him in case the figure they saw was still around and coming towards him. When he looked down, he saw Hope had reached the water's edge, but the bodies were being pulled out towards sea.

'We're going to lose them,' said Hope. 'I'm going to go in.'

'Wait,' shouted Macleod. 'You can't go in on that. Look at that tide. You'll get pulled out as well.'

Macleod scanned around him and could see lying up against

the rocks in the distance, a creel buoy, a marker that was left on top of the sea to show where creels, cages that would catch lobster and crab, were left on the sea floor. The buoy above would be attached to the creels by a rope line, and a coil of this rope was now lying up on the rocks with the buoy.

'Get that rope,' shouted Macleod as he continued to make his way down. 'Get that rope and I'll hang on to you when you go in.' By the time Macleod had reached the water's edge, Hope had returned with the rope, taken off her jeans, and begun to tie the rope around her.

'Here,' she said, handing the buoy end to Macleod.

'No risks. Don't want to lose you in the midst of this as well.'

Hope threw her leather jacket on the ground and dived into the water. Macleod watched as she fought the waves, struggling out. He thought at first that she was going to get thrown back onto the rocks, but slowly she made her way until she raised up one hand, indicating she'd reached a body.

Her hand lifted up, and she waved two fingers. Macleod reckoned she was tying something around the body, possibly the rope, and she swam again. She held up her hand, again with two fingers. Macleod watched as she tied something else. Then in the water, he saw both arms being raised, being swung towards him, which he took as an indication that he should pull.

Once he started, Hope began to swim in as well. It took several minutes before they pulled the bodies that were attached to the rope onto the shoreline. Macleod shifted a large rock onto the rope, hoping it would secure it before he reached down and pulled Hope from the water. She was frozen, and he saw her shiver as her bare legs came out of the water, her top drenched around her. She didn't hesitate,

186

reaching back into the water and pulling the first body ashore. A second body followed.

'That's Alexei,' said Hope. 'This one's Karina. They've killed all the sons. All the sons and their partners. And look, he's been stabbed—Alexei's been stabbed. And Karina as well.'

'Pull them further up. Make sure this water can't take them back. We'll tie the bodies up here, make sure we don't lose them back to the sea.'

Macleod looked up and saw a figure at the top of the cliff looking down at them. It seemed to turn and walk away. 'I'll get after it,' said Hope.

'No, you won't. Secure these bodies, then we climb up. We go together. We need to be careful, Hope. We're part of the plot of whatever game is being played. We're part of the story line. If we step outside of it, they may end us as well.'

Hope shivered. Macleod wasn't sure if it was from the water or from the thought of the murderer they were after.

'But Clarissa and Lyla, they're off at the beach house.'

'Help me drag these bodies up. Secure them. That's our first port of call.'

Chapter 23

C larissa continued to march through the driving wind and rain towards the beach house. In her wake, Lyla was complaining, but the woman was too petrified to go anywhere on her own. Clarissa ignored her, determined to just continue. Get to the beach house, find everyone, lock it down until Macleod came back with Hope. Maybe that's what would be required, just to sit this storm out somewhere. Put everyone together, maybe back at the breakfast room, where they were supposed to have lunch. Maybe in there everyone could sit, could sleep. Eyes on everyone until such time as they could get off the island.

As the beach house came into view, sharper now, in focus instead of a pale image in the driving rain, Clarissa looked to see if anyone was around it. There were no obvious figures, but she still approached cautiously before stepping up to the front door and rapping on it loudly.

'Frank, Sarah,' she shouted. 'Anyone there?' There was no reply. She tried to look in through some of the windows, but couldn't see much, and so knocked on the door again. After a moment, she saw Sarah emerge out into the main room, wrapped up in a dressing gown and rubbing her hair down with a towel.

'It all looks all right, then,' said Lyla. 'I mean, you don't go for a shower when you're in trouble, do you?'

'Just stay close,' said Clarissa. 'Assume nothing until we find out what's happening. Maybe Swen hasn't got here yet. Maybe he hasn't reached whoever else he's about to . . . Remember that nobody came. No Mischa, no Yulia, no Kira. Where is everyone?'

Sarah opened the door and looked with concern at Clarissa.

'What's the matter? You've got a face like, well, I don't know what. Something wrong?'

'Yes, everyone's missing. Has anybody been down here? Where's Frank?'

'Frank popped out. I don't know why. I assumed he just wanted to stretch his legs or something.'

That didn't make any sense to Clarissa. The man was petrified, worried. He went off to the beach house to hide. Why on earth would you turn round then and start going out for a walk on your own?

'Has anyone been here?' asked Clarissa.

'No,' said Sarah. 'I was just having a shower.'

A shower in the middle of the day? When you're worried about people being around? Clarissa thought this a little strange. It wasn't unreasonable, just a little odd.

'Let us in,' said Lyla. 'There's people out and about. People looking to . . . God, maybe kill people.'

'Calm down,' said Clarissa. 'We don't know if that's happening yet. We don't know what's happening. We'll just sit here. The inspector and the sergeant will be back here very shortly. Then we'll see the next way forward. People can't have gone far; it's not that big an island.'

189

'Of course, come in,' said Sarah. 'If you want, take a seat over there.' She pointed to the sofa in the front room of the beach house.

'But Frank isn't here,' confirmed Clarissa. 'I'll check his bedroom.'

Sarah nodded. Clarissa marched through, flung open the door and looked around the bedroom. It had a bed that had been slept in, but very little else. Frank had brought some of his clothing down with him, but not a lot, and there were certainly no marks that it had been lived in for a long time.

On return from the bedroom, Clarissa saw two worried faces.

'Sarah said she heard something outside,' said Lyla.

'Did you hear it?' asked Clarissa.

'No, but I was over here on this side of the room. Sarah said she heard it from out there.'

'Okay,' said Clarissa, walking to the windows and looking out into the driving rain again. 'I can't see anything. Maybe I'll go back to Frank's room and have a look.'

Clarissa tore back in, looked out of the bedroom window but again, could see nothing.

'What about yours?' she asked Sarah on return.

'It's on the wrong side. I wouldn't do it. It's that direction the sound came from,' she said. 'I wouldn't go into my bedroom in case they can see you through the window. Why don't you have a look outside? Pop around.'

Clarissa nodded but thought she should take it very carefully when she stepped outside. Slowly she opened the door and stood listening to the driving rain as it bounced off the roof. It was no pitter-patter, but a constant deluge. Carefully, she made her way to the end of the building, peeked quickly around

190

the side. It led to where Frank's bedroom window was, and Clarissa could see nothing.

The land around the beach house was fairly flat, and she couldn't see anyone there either, and so stalked to the end of this new side of the house. She kept looking back over her shoulder, worried in case somebody would be coming from behind her. With her back to the house, she walked sideways, looking here and there until she reached the corner.

Once again, she peeked around quickly. There was nothing. Now at the rear of the house, Clarissa thought it best if she picked up the pace and got back inside, but she couldn't see anything from this direction either. She sneaked along the back wall before reaching the apex, and throwing her head around for a quick look again, her mouth almost dropped.

On the ground, less than two feet away from her, under what would be Sarah's window, lay Swen. The big man had blood all over his neck and it was mixing in with the rain that was falling on his body. His clothes were soaked through, but his face had a look of almost contentment on it, the eyes closed, and his lips, not in a smile, but in a serene look, almost level.

Clarissa jumped back, automatically looked over her shoulder to see if anyone was there, before turning around and reaching down to Swen. She tried for a pulse in more than one area but found nothing. The man was still warm, so this had happened recently.

Clarissa ran back to the front of the house, banged on the door and watched as Lyla unlocked it. Stepping inside, her shawl dripping, Clarissa looked over at Sarah. The woman seemed to have glazed over, almost.

'Where's Frank?' asked Clarissa. When she got no answer, she stared intently at Sarah. The eyes were looking somewhere else. Sarah was somewhere else. Her mind was somewhere else.

'I said, "Where's Frank?"' asked Clarissa, stepping forward to shake the woman.

'Frank went for a walk. I told you.'

'What's up?' asked Lyla. 'What's up?' It was almost a shriek.

'Swen's outside. He's dead,' said Clarissa. 'It looks like somebody knifed him. Where's Frank?' asked Clarissa again.

'Frank's okay,' said Sarah. 'He's okay.'

Clarissa went to barge past Sarah to reach for her room, but suddenly the woman pulled a knife on her, and Clarissa took a step back. Over her shoulder, Lyla screamed. 'There's no need for that,' said Clarissa. 'There's no need. Put the knife down.'

'There's every need. It had to be done. Swen had to die.'

'But what about the others?' asked Clarissa. 'Why kill the Duke?'

'It had to be done. I needed to do it. I needed it for what I want. Don't you understand?'

Sarah lunged forward with the knife, causing Clarissa to step back. She reached up, unpinned the brooch that held her shawl around her and let the brooch fall to the ground. Grabbing the shawl off her shoulders, she held it with two hands in front of her like some sort of mad Scottish matador's cape. Sarah took a large swipe well clear of Clarissa, who stepped back once more.

'You need to understand. It's the only way. It's the only way to get what I want. The Duke wouldn't give me it.'

'But why Victor? What does Victor have to do with it? I'm puzzled.'

Sarah's face seemed at first confused but then she stared coldly at Clarissa. She saw there were almost tears in Sarah's eyes.

'Had to be done for what I wanted. Had to be. Had to be done or else.'

'Or else what?' asked Clarissa. 'Or else what?'

There was a sudden glance from Sarah, looking back towards her bedroom. Clarissa seized the opportunity and made a run for the bedroom, holding out her shawl in front of her. Sarah lashed out quickly, the knife catching in the shawl. Clarissa wrapped it around the arm of Sarah as best she could. But Sarah was younger, and despite having one arm trapped, she caught Clarissa with an almighty slap across the face. It was quite a shock. The last thing Clarissa expected was a slap and not a punch.

Clarissa was also still hanging onto the shawl which was now caught up in the knife, and it caused Clarissa to spin, fall onto her bottom and then roll over, the shawl now gone.

'Watch out,' screamed Lyla, and made for the door. Clarissa could hear it open and shut as she desperately tried to get back to her feet, but Sarah came over, knife raised above her head. She jumped forward, pushing Clarissa back down to the floor. She fought with an arm up in front of her, caught Sarah's shoulder, and watched as she raised the knife above her head.

'Had to be done for what I wanted. It had to be done for what I wanted. Do you understand? Do you understand?'

'Don't do it,' shouted Clarissa, her blood running cold, as she realised she wasn't strong enough to hold the woman off her. Clarissa could handle people, but from a distance, not when she was surprised like this, not when they had just been thrust upon her. She was older now, older than when she'd started, days when she could take the rough and tumble a lot more than she could now. Now she had to be ready for it, ahead of the game. *Think smart*, she thought to herself. *Fight smart, Clarissa.* She reached up, grabbed Sarah's face, thrust her finger into one eye, but the woman was possessed. The knife was raised.

The door was suddenly flung open. In the corner of her eye Clarissa saw a streak of red hair and a tall body flew past her face, kicking Sarah off to one side. Behind, a shorter man ran after the sergeant, throwing himself down onto the ground on top of the two women. As Clarissa tried to sit up, she saw Macleod and Hope force the knife from Sarah's hand, and together they turned her over, placing handcuffs on her wrists behind her back.

'Are you okay?' asked Macleod. 'Urquhart, are you okay?'

'Fine,' she said. 'Fine. She didn't get a blow in.'

'Good,' said Macleod.

'Swen's outside,' said Clarissa.

'So is Lyla. She's running around. We best get her back,' said Macleod.

'No, no, Seoras. Swen's dead. I think Sarah killed him.'

Clarissa could see the confusion on Macleod's face. 'I was trying to go into that room. She stopped me. She was worried I was going to enter her room.'

Macleod stood up, letting Hope maintain her grip on Sarah. He walked to the door and opened it, stepped inside, and Clarissa rose to her feet as she saw the look of disbelief on his face. She staggered over, out of breath, adrenaline pumping through her body, placed her hand on Macleod's shoulder as she looked around the room. Sitting on the floor, hands tied behind her back, feet tied together, with a gag in her mouth, was Mischa. Beside her in the same position was her daughter

Kira. On the other side of the bed was Frank, tied up exactly the same.

'I don't believe it,' said Macleod in a whisper to Clarissa. 'I don't believe it.'

'I didn't see that one coming, Seoras. We'd best untie them though.'

Clarissa stepped forward, still out of breath, still feeling the blood pulsing through her body, but it was over. It was finally over. She reached down and undid the gag around Mischa's mouth, turned around and undid Kira's too. Then she undid Mischa's wrists, left her to undo her own feet as she started to undo Kira's. There was a muffled sound from the other side of the room, and Clarissa saw that Frank was still tied up, desperately urging someone to free him. Looking back over her shoulder, Clarissa saw Macleod still standing, almost in disbelief.

'Seoras? Probably should, you know, untie Frank.'

There wasn't even an acknowledgement. Instead, Macleod walked around, still as if he was looking off into the distance. He undid the man's binds and then completely ignored him, as Frank gave a thanks.

'Insane bitch, totally insane bitch,' said Frank. 'Can you believe that? I mean, why? What's she up to?'

'Her hatred for my husband must have run deep, to want to kill off his family as well. Well done, Inspector, well done. You've probably saved our lives,' said Mischa.

Macleod looked over, gave a shake of his head, and walked out of the room.

'Is your inspector always like this?' Mischa asked Clarissa.

'No,' said Clarissa. 'He's only like this when the job's on.'

'But he's done it,' said Mischa. 'He's found our killer.'

195

'No,' said Clarissa. 'No, he hasn't.'

Chapter 24

Macleod sat in the large dining hall, staring over at Mischa, who was talking to servants, making sure that dinner was served. Beside Macleod, Hope seemed restless, as if she wanted to get out of the place.

'Don't seem so uneasy,' said Macleod.

'I am uneasy. You're telling me we've got the wrong person. You're telling me that we've still got a killer here and at the moment we can't touch them. But more than that, we're going to leave.'

'Yes. We've been asked to leave because our job is done,' said Macleod. 'We've played our part. I always wondered what part I was here to play. I always wondered why we were called into a place where I wasn't allowed to exercise my normal jurisdiction. Well, I know now.'

'What?' asked Hope.

'For validation, so the world can sit and say, 'Macleod says it was a such and such person. He found her. Therefore, that's who it was. For the world to look at.'

'But it wasn't her, was it?'

'Oh, I believe she killed Swen. She may have had help, though, but she killed Swen and I believe she was coerced into it.'

'Do you still believe it was Mischa?' said Hope in a whisper.

'No. Well, not at the head of it all. Mischa runs around and does everything, but there's somebody beyond Mischa. You see, Hope, the game plan's not over yet. It's barely begun. I didn't see it for a long while, but I do now.'

'What do you mean?'

'Well, this has actually all been about family. We've been looking at guests and that, but the guests are under control. Frank was here in what was a dangerous situation, so dangerous that he hired Swen to look after him. Well, then Frank must have been paid to come here, because otherwise, why would he come? So, he's under control. Lyla and Sarah, they came to the family for things. They were used to some degree by the Duke, but also by the family.

'We saw Lyla, the way she reacted. The guests didn't know what was going on. They were frightened. They're here because they're made to be here. Lyla broke off affairs with the Duke and yet is still here with Mischa around. Even after the Duke dies? I'd have been out of here like a shot. There was still time then. The boat was still running.'

'If it's about the family, why are we here?'

'The way they run it over in Zupci is that men are in charge. Well, they'd be in charge until there was only a woman left, then the woman would have to be in charge, but the women are really in charge anyway.'

'What do you mean?' asked Hope. 'You're losing me on this one.'

'Just because somebody says they're the head of something doesn't mean they are. Look at the Duke. After all these affairs and other depravities, Mischa is still beside him. Mischa doesn't mess about like that. The Duke is Yulia's son, so Mischa's come in from the outside. She's been brought in to handle him. I learned as much when they talked about Alexei's wife, Karina, or Karen. She came in and was meant to get a hold of Alexei, but he still wasn't the business.

'This is about where the future of the family goes. They're just taking over that country. They're in charge. They're going to have to stamp their authority on it. Suddenly you go from a much smaller ring of influence to a big international ring. Clearly, the country has things that other countries want. Our government's a testimony to that, but who's going to run things? The Duke is somebody who played around with actresses, glamour models. He's not the right sort, so you get rid of him. Then it falls to the sons after that. Victor, well, Victor's just a mess. He's not going to be able to run anything. Alexei, they hoped would. That's why he's been married to Karina, but he's not there either. Hasn't worked. And as for Pavel . . . '

'Mischa killed her own sons? She killed her family and her sons? But she couldn't do. We know Mischa was with Lyla. She couldn't have killed Pavel.'

'She didn't kill Pavel. Pavel's her boy. Pavel was the one she wanted. For all his strangeness, he's really a poor soul, isn't he? Mischa didn't blame him. The other two, she blamed. They had everything going for them, but she didn't blame Pavel. He was a poor soul, never really taken in hand and shown how he should be. Left as the castoff runt of the family, running around, doing what he wanted. I reckon he might even have picked out Julie McGeehan when asked what instructor he wanted. Pavel then makes a grab for her.

'And there's the letching of the other men. We've gone

through many cases where these men, ones who think they own women, can do what they want with them. Well, I think some women bit back.'

'What do we do with Mischa? If you think she's done it.'

'What do I do? What can I do?' said Macleod. 'I haven't got the evidence to do it. Circumstantially, how does the Duke get stabbed coming in from above? He's utterly naked as well. That's because Mischa has done it during their lovemaking. She's taken him outside, killed him in the middle of it, throwing him off the cliff, down into the sea.'

'And the knife, you think the knife is the same? The one that killed Swen and Lyla that Sarah used?' asked Hope.

'It probably is.'

'The only thing I don't get is who killed Pavel if Mischa didn't. If Mischa is so hell-bent on running the family, who killed Pavel? You said she couldn't do it.'

'It was Yulia,' said Macleod.

'Yulia? You said Yulia couldn't kill anyone.'

'Not directly. Who's going to take over the family?'

'Well, Mischa. Mischa is clearly the lead.'

'Mischa is not of the family, Hope. It'll be Kira.'

'Kira killed her own brother?'

'You see Kira? The Duke died, she's in black, like Mischa. She's alongside Yulia. Yulia got Kira to kill Pavel. Yulia has been prepping her since she realised that the family men didn't cut it. She's only just coming of age now, at a point where she could run the business, guided by Yulia.'

'But Mischa is in the way.'

'Yes,' said Macleod. 'Yes, she is.' He stood up and walked across the room to Mischa. She held out her hand.

'You'll forgive me if I don't shake it,' said Macleod. 'You

see, you can put me in these trappings, all the money around here, all the artwork, everything else, all the supposed Royal Family finery, but deep down, you're just gangsters, and I recognise you. Sophisticated, loaded with money and with high influence. Still the same down below, though.'

'I take it you won't be telling your government that, though,' said Mischa. 'After all, you'll look ridiculous.'

'You knew I would, and you did everything to stop me running a proper investigation. Yes, you said your husband had died. That was the reason, had to treat guests properly. Foreign ways and all that. Every stage you played me like a puppet and that's been the whole point. To have me come in and say to the world, "Look, we found our killer." What's going to happen then? I'm sure you'll smooth it all over with our government.'

'Sarah's become a Zupci national, I think you'll find, with diplomatic status,' said Mischa. 'She'll head back to Zupci. Yes, there'll be a trial. She has diplomatic status, so it can't be here, and she'll get to be what she used to be. It's funny how some people crave that, isn't it? She wanted the glamour back. She enjoyed prostrating herself in front of people. So much so that she actually held the knife with me when we stabbed Swen, but you guessed that, didn't you?'

'And Frank, you'd already tied him up, hadn't you?'

'Relationships with my husband and Frank were far too cordial. Frank needed to be put in his place. Oh, he was here because he knew he had to be, or we were coming elsewhere. He knew the alternative was worse. No doubt he tried to drop things subtly to yourself. He understands now that if he does step out of line, what will happen. You see, family is no sentimental thing to me. Family is the business. Even if our

201

own family members don't line up to the business, they don'
stick around.'

Macleod shook his head. 'Even Pavel, although you couldn'
do that yourself, could you?'

Macleod saw the tear in the eye and watched as the woman
fought to hold it back. She was strong, he realised, very strong
Brutal people are not always strong, but she was.

'And that tells me that you have a master,' he continued. 'You
may have done and organised most of this, but they're the one
on top. The thing is, Mischa, and I mean this quite sincerely
you're not family. Be very wary because you're next.'

'You're wrong, Inspector. The business is now mine.'

Macleod reached down and picked up a small canape from
the table and popped it in his mouth. 'I'll be going in about
he looked at his watch, 'half an hour, and I'm done with thi
place. I'm going up back home to try and help my partne
recover from a trauma people visited on us. You've wasted
my time being here. You've wasted my colleagues' time. Tha
is what I'll be telling my government. Like I say, watch you
back. This isn't over.'

'Are you threatening me?' asked Mischa.

'No. I'm out,' said Macleod. 'But watch your back. It's th
friendly bit of advice I shouldn't be giving you.'

With that, Macleod turned away, walked back to Hope an
told her to come pick up her bags from her room. As he left th
dining room, he stopped at the double doors, turned back an
looked over at Mischa. She looked back at him, eyes focuse
on him, and he could tell that her mind was racing.

He turned and walked away along the corridors, back to hi
room to finish off the last of his luggage. He knew it was th
last time he'd ever see her.

Epilogue

Macleod sat in the sunshine with a lemonade in the glass beside him. Across from him, Jane was lying in the sun, glass of wine beside her and he realised she'd come on so much in these last few weeks. It had been nearly a month since he was on the island of Mingulay. After talking to the foreign office during several long meetings in which he'd explained his position, he'd returned to normal duties. They'd accepted what he'd said, but they hadn't given an explanation on why they allowed themselves to become involved in this rather dubious way.

Macleod didn't care, didn't want to know, just wanted to make sure that his own country understood what was going on. As far as he was concerned, it was case closed. He'd done his duty. Completed what they'd asked of him. Now he was back serving the people he should've been serving, the good folk of the highlands and islands.

The doorbell rang and Macleod looked over at Jane, who looked back at him. 'You expecting anyone, Seoras?' she asked.

'No,' he said.

'Well, it's a nice day. If it's important, they'll come round to the back.'

'Yes,' he said. 'If it's important.' He sat back in the chair and hoped it wasn't important. They could do with an afternoon together, an afternoon of doing nothing, an afternoon of recovery. An afternoon when the world could just go and get stuffed.

The doorbell rang two more times before he heard the crunch of the stones, and someone coming round the path at the side of the house.

'It's you,' said Jane. 'Come on. Come on in.'

'Don't get up. I'm just here for five minutes to see him.'

'Well, he is here,' said Macleod, knowing that he was currently out of sight of McGrath as she made it to the rear patio. He turned and smiled in the sunshine as the taller sergeant walked over to him. Behind her, he could see John, Hope's partner.

'Well, come on in,' said Jane to John. 'Come and sit down.'

'No,' said Hope. 'We're off hours. You guys need your time and I just had to bring him this.'

'Bring me what?' asked Macleod. 'Telling me this couldn't wait for the office?'

'You don't read your internet, so no, it couldn't. Here.'

From behind her back Hope pulled out a newspaper. She threw it down on the table and turned over two pages. There was an article that was ringed in red pen. The headline said, 'Tragic death of Zupci widow.' Macleod leaned forward and read the text beneath. Mischa had been found dead, having died in a Jacuzzi in an electrical accident.

'You called it?'

'Yes. Yes, I did,' said Macleod. 'Yulia. Yulia's the family there. Yulia's the driving force, but she's going to make sure that Kira is, too.'

204

'But what about Mischa? Mischa was doing everything she asked.'

'No, not when it came to Pavel,' said Macleod. 'It was a weakness the family couldn't have, not with their head. The head of the family has to be able to do anything, and Kira proved herself,' said Macleod.

'Are you going to tell them?'

'Tell who?' said Macleod.

'The government who sent you there.'

'I already have. I told them this would happen. We've been waiting for it.'

'So that's that,' said Hope.

'That's that,' said Macleod. 'Sometimes, you don't get justice. You need to understand that, Hope. Sometimes, there's things you can't do. I did what I could. I warned Mischa. I told my government. Let's just get back to being police officers. Let's just get back to looking after the highlands and islands.'

'And just you get back to taking out John wherever you were going,' said Jane.

Hope picked up the paper, put it under her arm, and turned away. 'I'll see you in the office.'

'See you there,' said Macleod. 'And Hope! Let it go. It was a rogues' gallery to begin with. I'm not sure what justice would have looked like anyway.'

Macleod sat back in his chair and closed his eyes, and he heard Hope leave, a goodbye from John to Jane, and then after a few minutes, he heard Jane wander over towards his chair.

'You're very good to that girl,' said Jane.

'Aye,' said Macleod.

'Because you're more hacked off at this than she'll ever be, and you didn't show one ounce of it.'

'True,' said Macleod. 'True, but she's going to have to be better than me, so I have to pretend, at least.'

He felt Jane's hands on his shoulders, rubbing them gently, and then a kiss on the forehead before she wandered back over to lie down again in the sun. *She'll be better than me*, he said to himself and felt his right hand clench in a fist. Yulia Zupci was a name he would not forget.

Read on to discover the Patrick
Smythe series!

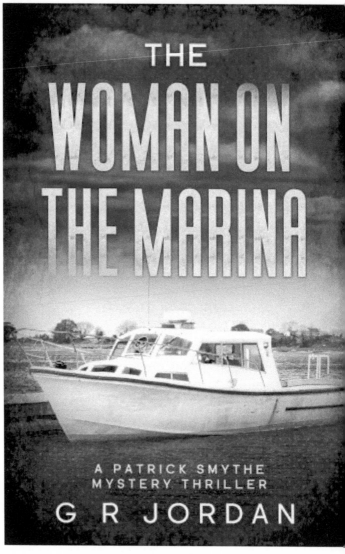

Start your Patrick Smythe journey here!

Patrick Smythe is a former Northern Irish policeman wh

after suffering an amputation after a bomb blast, takes to the sea between the west coast of Scotland and his homeland to ply his trade as a private investigator. Join Paddy as he tries to work to his own ethics while knowing how to bend the rules he once enforced. Working from his beloved motorboat 'Craigantlet', Paddy decides to rescue a drug mule in this short story from the pen of G R Jordan.

Join G R Jordan's monthly newsletter about forthcoming releases and special writings for his tribe of avid readers and then receive your free Patrick Smythe short story.

Go to https://bit.ly/PatrickSmythe for your Patrick Smythe journey to start!

About the Author

GR Jordan is a self-published author who finally decided at forty that in order to have an enjoyable lifestyle, his creative beast within would have to be unleashed. His books mirror that conflict in life where acts of decency contend with self-promotion, goodness stares in horror at evil, and kindness blindsides us when we at our worst. Corrupting our world with his parade of wondrous and horrific characters, he highlights everyday tensions with fresh eyes whilst taking his methodical, intelligent mainstays on a roller-coaster ride of dilemmas, all the while suffering the banter of their provocative sidekicks.

A graduate of Loughborough University where he masqueraded as a chemical engineer but ultimately played American football, Gary had worked at changing the shape of cereal flakes and pulled a pallet truck for a living. Watching vegetables freeze at -40'C was another career highlight and he was also one of the Scottish Highlands "blind" air traffic controllers.

These days he has graduated to answering a telephone to people in trouble before telephoning other people to sort it out.

Having flirted with most places in the UK, he is now based in the Isle of Lewis in Scotland where his free time is spent between raising a young family with his wife, writing, figuring out how to work a loom and caring for a small flock of chickens. Luckily, his writing is influenced by his varied work and life experience as the chickens have not been the poetical inspiration he had hoped for!

You can connect with me on:
- https://grjordan.com
- https://facebook.com/carpetlessleprechaun

Subscribe to my newsletter:
- https://bit.ly/PatrickSmythe

Also by G R Jordan

G R Jordan writes across multiple genres including crime, dark and action adventure fantasy, feel good fantasy, mystery thriller and horror fantasy. Below is a selection of his work. Whilst all books are available across online stores, signed copies are available at his personal shop.

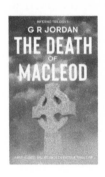

**The Death of Macleod - Inferno Book 1
A slaughter of innocents. A crazed public demands vengeance from any source. Can Macleod hold his poise amidst a cry for blood before justice?**

When a heinous crime against children pro-vokes a national outcry, Detective Inspector Macleod and his team are under pressure for results like never before. As the murders continue, top brass demands a scapegoat at all costs. But when Detective Sergeant McGrath suspects evidence has been planted to sate the public's bloodlust, can Macleod find the real killer before the public tears their sacrificial lamb apart?

Today in the crucible, tomorrow the gallows.

Busman's Holiday (A Kirsten Stewart Thriller #8)

https://grjordan.com/product/busmans-holiday

Kirsten seeks romance and sun on leaving the service. A chance encounter leaves her partner in the middle of a kidnapping. Can Kirsten find her beloved before a terrorist executes him in the name of freedom?

When Kirsten and Craig take a sun drenched holiday in an attempt to cement their love, little do they suspect their quaint destination will become part of a country's nightmare. The black hand rises, murdering a local mayor, and takes Craig hostage, forcing Kirsten to become a merciless rescuer once again. With no back-up, in a land she doesn't understand, the service's black sheep must curry favours and avoid the local police as she brings down a country's dark underbelly.

How dark your passions when your soul is uneasy!

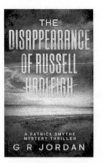

The Disappearance of Russell Hadleigh (Patrick Smythe Book 1)

https://grjordan.com/product/the-disappearance-of-russell-hadleigh

A retired judge fails to meet his golf partner. His wife calls for help while running a fantasy play ring. When Russians start co-opting into a fairly traded clothing brand, can Paddy untangle the strands before the bodies start littering the golf course?

In his first full novel, Patrick Smythe, the single-armed former policeman, must infiltrate the golfing social scene to discover the fate of his client's husband. Assisted by a young starlet of the greens, Paddy tries to understand just who bears a grudge and who likes to play in the rough, culminating in a high stakes showdown where lives are hanging by the reaction of a moment. If you love pacey action, suspicious motives and devious characters, then Paddy Smythe operates amongst your kind of people.

Love is a matter of taste but money always demands more of its suitor.

Lightning Source UK Ltd.
Milton Keynes UK
UKHW031018190922
409092UK00001B/250

9 781915 562100